TOO TALL TO VAULT

Monica looked down at Kelly. She remembered when they had been the same height. "Is gymnastics what's really important, Kel?" she asked. "I mean, I can't even do a simple squat vault. I'm off balance on the beam, I almost killed myself on the uneven parallel bars last week, and . . . I don't know."

"Oh, Monica," Kelly began. "You just have to—"

"But at Dr. Thayer's," Monica interrupted, "I can do everything right. It isn't difficult. And it doesn't take hours and days and weeks of practice. It makes me think I can do anything and be good at it."

Kelly gazed at Monica earnestly. "You *can* do anything. You're already good at gymnastics, Monica, and if—"

"Kelly, I'm not. Don't you see? I *used* to be good at gymnastics, but not anymore. And I might never be again. Maybe I should try to be good at something else."

Kelly's eyes widened. "Something else? What are you saying? Are you quitting SGA?"

Be sure to read all the exciting
AMERICAN GOLD GYMNASTS
titles from Bantam Books:

#1 Competition Fever
#2 Balancing Act
#3 Split Decision

and coming soon:

#4 The Bully Coach

AMERICAN GOLD GYMNASTS

by Gabrielle Charbonnet

Split Decision

BANTAM BOOKS
NEW YORK • TORONTO • LONDON • SYDNEY • AUCKLAND

RL 5, 008–012
SPLIT DECISION
A Bantam Skylark Book / July 1996

*Skylark Books is a registered trademark of Bantam Books,
a division of Bantam Doubleday Dell Publishing Group, Inc.
Registered in U.S. Patent and Trademark Office and elsewhere.*

Series design: Madalina Stefan

ISBN 0-553-48298-X

Published simultaneously in the United States and Canada.

Bantam Books are published by Bantam Books, a division of
Bantam Doubleday Dell Publishing Group, Inc. Its trademark,
consisting of the words "Bantam Books" and the portrayal of a
rooster, is Registered in U.S. Patent and Trademark Office and in
other countries. Marca Registrada. Bantam Books, 1540 Broadway,
New York, New York 10036.

PRINTED IN THE UNITED STATES OF AMERICA

OPM   0 9 8 7 6 5 4 3 2 1

Split Decision

Chapter One

"Does everyone understand what to do?" Dimitri Resnikov asked in his deep voice.

Monica Hales and the five other members of her team, the Silver Stars, nodded. This Thursday afternoon, Dimitri, their head coach, was teaching them a new vaulting mount.

"First you will run down this line of floor mats to build momentum," Dimitri said, gesturing with his hand. "Then you'll begin your roundoff here, where I've put this piece of masking tape. If you're tall, like Monica, begin a bit earlier. If you're smaller, like Harry, begin a tiny bit later."

Monica glanced across at her best friend, Kelly Reynolds, and saw her grin. Monica frowned. At twelve years old, she was one of the tallest gymnasts at SGA—Sugarloaf Gymnastic Academy, the gymnastics training center that Kelly's mother,

Emma Stanton, owned in the Sugarloaf suburb of Atlanta. Dimitri had married Emma almost three months before, so he was Kelly's new stepfather. His daughter, Maya Resnikov, who was also a Silver Star, was Kelly's stepsister.

Now Monica groaned quietly and brushed a strand of hair off her forehead. "I told you," she whispered to Kelly. "I'm going to grow myself right out of a gymnastics career."

Kelly shrugged, paying attention to Dimitri.

Monica knew Kelly didn't think being a tall, slim African American girl was something to complain about. That was because Kelly was tiny and wiry—the perfect build for a gymnast. Everyone knew that gymnastic moves were easier if you were small and compact, and Kelly was the second-smallest Silver Star. Only Hiroko Kobayashi, whom everyone called Harry, was smaller.

Harry's only eleven, Monica thought. *But even so, she probably won't get much taller. With my luck I'll probably end up being six feet tall or something. The perfect height for a . . . basketball player.* Monica had no plans to be a professional basketball player. Gymnastics was practically her whole life—though lately it seemed harder than ever.

"It will take practice before you know exactly

where to begin your roundoff," Dimitri continued, snapping Monica out of her daydream. "After your roundoff, you will land on this bank of safety mats. Every single roundoff must be exactly the same. Your heels must be in the exact same place on the springboard each time."

"That's impossible," Candace Stiles said. She shook her head, and her curly red ponytail bounced.

"Nothing is impossible, Candace," Dimitri said with a smile, "if you practice it enough. And this mount is very important. Without it, you cannot perform many Olympic-level vaults."

"Like the Yerchenko," Harry pointed out.

"That's correct," Dimitri said in his accented English.

"Don't worry. You'll be able to do it, Candace," Maya said encouragingly. "I bet you'll get a lot of power, too."

Monica saw Candace's face relax. Maya had said the right thing.

"Once your roundoffs are perfected, we'll practice adding a back handspring," Dimitri went on. "Then we'll put both elements together so that your back handspring lands on top of the vaulting horse. And you'll be halfway to a Yerchenko."

Kelly shifted her feet, excited. "That'll be so great," she said. "I can't wait till we try it. Do you think we'll have learned the complete Yerchenko in time for the exhibition at Forest Park?"

Forest Park was the local high school hosting this year's Fitness Week exhibition. In about three weeks, there would be demonstrations of cheerleading, dance, tennis, karate, horseback riding— almost every sport anyone could think of. SGA was in charge of the gymnastics demonstration.

"I don't think so, Kellinka," Dimitri said honestly, using his Russian nickname for Kelly. "But Emma will work with you to create a special routine for Forest Park."

"My brother Gene is going to be in the tennis demonstration for Sugarloaf High," Monica said.

"I thought Gene was a total computer-head," Kathryn Stiles said. Kathryn was Candace's fraternal twin. Though Candace's hair was bright red, hers was auburn. Candace's eyes were green, Kathryn's hazel. And Candace was outgoing and carefree, while Kathryn was quieter and a hardworking student both at school and at SGA.

"My brother *is* a computer geek," Monica said. "But he's also good at tennis. Maybe it's because he's six feet tall."

"Excuse me, Dimitri," Emma said, coming over to them. "There's a telephone call for you. Can you take it?"

Dimitri smiled at his wife, and Emma blushed happily. Kelly and Maya automatically looked at each other, grinned, and rolled their eyes. They loved to tease their parents about being honeymooners, but Monica knew that Kelly and Maya were glad Emma and Dimitri had found each other.

Monica thought their story was very romantic. Emma and Dimitri had first met in 1972, when they had both been competing in the Olympics. Emma had been only fourteen and on the United States team, and Dimitri had been eighteen and on the team for what was then the Soviet Union. Emma had won a silver medal for the vault in women's gymnastics, and Dimitri had come in fourth on the still rings—just a few hundredths of a point short of getting a medal.

Then they hadn't seen each other for twenty years. Emma had married Kelly's father, but they had divorced when Kelly was two years old. Kelly hadn't seen her father since then. Dimitri had married Maya's mother, but she had died of a blood disease when Maya was seven. Emma and Dimitri had met again when they were both coaching gymnasts competing in the World Championships. This time they had fallen in love. Almost three months ago, they had gotten married. Now Kelly had a stepfather, Maya had a stepmother, and Kelly and Maya each had a stepsister. It was like a fairy tale.

"Yes, dear," Dimitri told Emma gently. "I'll

take the call. Silvers, continue practicing your roundoffs. I won't be long." Dimitri took Emma's hand, and they walked toward the offices at the front of SGA.

Monica watched as they passed a group of Gold Stars working on the uneven parallel bars with the assistant coach, Susan Lu. At SGA, the very youngest students were called the Twinklers. Then there were the Copper Stars, the Bronze Stars, the Silver Stars, and the Gold Stars. The Silver Stars were eleven- to thirteen-year-olds. The Gold Stars, the most elite group at SGA, were fourteen years old and up. Most of them were aiming for the Olympics, though for the first time since Emma had opened the school, none had qualified for the current games.

"Speaking of tennis, did y'all see that tournament last night on TV?" Kathryn asked. "It was great."

"But why do the players grunt when they hit the ball?" Maya asked. "It sounds awful."

Kelly laughed. "I heard that it helps them hit harder or something. Personally, I'd rather be a gymnast. We're powerful but we're never noisy."

"Sometimes when I play tennis with Gene, I make sounds," Monica admitted. "When I really whack the ball."

"Maybe you should try grunting now," Candace teased. "It might help your roundoff."

Monica laughed. "Okay, I will. And after you see my roundoff, you'll take up grunting too."

Monica walked down to the end of the floor mats, almost forty feet away. She stood at the edge, and an intense look of concentration came over her face. She had been studying gymnastics since she was eight years old, and people had always said she was a natural at it. But lately something was wrong. Moves that had been easy last year now seemed more difficult. She felt clumsier—awkward. She suspected she knew the reason: her height. In the past year, she had grown almost four inches—an inch and a half of that over the last three months. Her sleeves were suddenly too short, her shoes too small. Her skirts were shorter than they were supposed to be, too. Kelly had even commented that Monica was as tall as Emma now. And Emma was a grown-up!

Monica began to run toward the springboard. Her hot pink, long-sleeved leotard glowed as she raced down the mats. Right before the masking-tape mark on the floor, she bounded into her roundoff. Starting with a cartwheel, she snapped her heels together in midair and brought them down hard.

"Ow!" she cried. She had started her roundoff

too late, and only her toes hit the edge of the springboard. She didn't bounce at all, but fell awkwardly back onto the high pile of safety mats.

"Meow!"

Monica felt her face burn with embarrassment as Kelly hurried toward her.

Chapter Two

"Monica," Kelly said, helping her stand. "Are you okay? We told you to grunt, not meow."

"I didn't meow," Monica said, brushing off her hands. "Y'all must be hearing things." Glaring at the springboard, she said, "I sure messed that up."

"You just started a little too late," Kelly said sympathetically. "Try it again, but start a good six inches before the mark. Are you sure you didn't hurt your feet?"

"No, I'm fine," Monica said. "I just feel stupid."

"Don't worry about it," Harry said. "You'll nail it next time."

Monica gave Harry a little smile. She had to snap out of her negative attitude. Emma always said that maintaining a good mental outlook was one of the most important skills a gymnast could have.

"Your turn," she said to Kelly. "Give us a good 'Unh!' "

Laughing, Kelly walked to the end of the mats. Monica could see her friend focusing her thoughts. Then Kelly ran fast toward the springboard. Right on the mark she went into her roundoff, snapping her feet down.

"Unh!" she cried, unable to suppress a giggle. The springboard gave under her weight, then popped back as Kelly shot high into the air. Monica shook her head. Kelly had done it perfectly, whereas Monica had looked like a Twinkler. Then Kelly was arching backward to land on the safety mats with a thud.

"Meow!"

The Silvers looked at Kelly in surprise as she scrambled to her feet.

"Even I heard that meow," Monica said. "Get up, Kel, and let's see where it's coming from."

The six Silver Stars each grabbed a thick mat, and together the girls pulled them apart.

"Nothing," Kelly reported, peering between the mats and on the floor around them. "Oh, wait a minute."

Monica gave a big heave and pulled a mat farther out. "I see it!" she cried. "Kelly, it's right there."

While Kelly held back a mat, Monica carefully reached down and cupped her hands around a tiny, dirty ball of fur. She stood up and opened her palms. A small pink mouth appeared. "Mew!"

"It's a kitten," Candace said in wonder.

"Really?" Kathryn said. "What was your first clue?"

"Oh, poor thing," Monica cooed. "Kelly, look—it must be sick." The kitten was in bad shape. Its fur was dirty and matted. Its eyes were crusty. And they could see its tiny ribs sticking out.

"Poor thing," Kelly echoed Monica. "How did it get in here? It could have been killed under the mats. Let's ask Emma what to do."

Just then Dimitri came back and clapped his hands. "All right," he said, "who has gone?"

"Dimitri, look," Kelly said, pointing to Monica's hands. "We found this kitten under the mats."

"Under the mats?" Dimitri repeated, peering at the tiny animal. "How did it get in here?"

"I don't know," Kelly said. "But we have to do something. It's sick."

Dimitri nodded. "Have you two done your roundoffs?"

Kelly and Monica nodded. *If you could call mine a roundoff,* Monica thought sourly.

"Take the kitten to Emma and ask her what to do. The rest of the Silvers, come practice your vaulting mounts." He waved at Harry, Maya, Candace, and Kathryn, and they all trotted back to the springboard.

Kelly and Monica found Emma with Susan Lu, coaching the Gold Stars on the uneven parallel bars.

"Don't look," Kelly whispered. "Beau Jarrett, two o'clock."

Monica snapped her head to the right. Sure enough, there was Beau Jarrett, one of the few male Gold Stars. He was working on the even parallel bars, an event for men only. Even though he was older—sixteen—Monica had a killer crush on him.

"Good thing you had that pacemaker installed," Kelly whispered. "Otherwise you'd probably have heart failure."

Monica nodded absently, then got what Kelly was saying. "Fine—make fun of me," she said as Kelly giggled. "Someday the thunderbolt will hit *you*. Then see how sympathetic I am."

Kelly grinned.

"What's up, girls?" Emma said, keeping one eye on Randi Marshall, who was on the bars.

"Emma, we found this kitten," Kelly said. At home she called Emma Mom, but here she called her Emma like everyone else. "Under the mats."

"My goodness," Emma said, looking at the kitten shivering in Monica's hands. "Poor baby! I know—why don't you take it to that new veterinary clinic a few stores down? I think it's called Fur, Feather, and Scale. They'll know what to do."

"Great, thanks, Emma," Monica said. "Come on, Kelly."

"Hang on—Kelly, could I talk to you in my office for a minute?" Emma asked. "Monica can take the kitten by herself. And Monica—put on some shoes before you go out."

Monica looked down and wiggled her bare toes. "Oops! I almost forgot. Guess I'll see you later, Kel."

Kelly nodded. "Yeah, at Gianelli's," she said. Gianelli's was an ice cream parlor a few stores down. The Silver Stars often met there after class.

Monica quickly headed back to the girls' locker room, cradling the kitten against her chest. *I'm so glad to be getting out of class,* she thought, feeling a little guilty. *Today just isn't going well.*

"Gold Stars, take a water break now," she heard Emma say.

13

Have I done anything wrong? Kelly wondered as she sat down in the chair across from her mother's desk. She racked her brain, but nothing came to mind. She and Maya had been getting along great. When Maya had first come, Kelly had thought she was stuck-up and unfriendly. Maya had thought Kelly was a spoiled American snob. They had both been wrong. Once they had made up, they had made up for good. So why did Emma want to talk to her?

"As you know," Emma began, sitting behind her desk, "we've had a large increase in students since Dimitri came. Right now we're looking for another full-time coach."

Kelly nodded. Lately she and Maya had more responsibilities at home because Emma and Dimitri were working so many hours. Kelly had made dinner twice in the last week. Once she had ordered takeout pizza, and once she had made tunafish salad.

"Yes, well, Dimitri and I have talked about it, and we've decided to ask you if you could help us here at SGA," Emma continued. "By coaching the Twinklers and getting them ready for Fitness Week."

Kelly was so surprised she just stared at her mother. Coach the Twinklers! Her? She was only a Silver Star!

"You know they come twice a week for forty-five minutes. It would mean giving up your Monday and Friday afternoons—so your week would be really full, since you have your Silvers classes Tuesday, Wednesday, Thursday, and Saturday."

"Hmm," Kelly said, thinking. On Mondays and Fridays, she sometimes came to SGA anyway, to hang out and watch the Gold Stars, or to practice on whatever equipment wasn't being used. But sometimes she and Monica or Maya hung out at home or went to the mall. If she coached the Twinklers, she wouldn't be able to do that.

"It would just be until the exhibition at Fitness Week," Emma said. "By then we should have another full-time coach, and you could have your Mondays and Fridays back. But I don't want to pressure you. If you would rather not do it, that's fine." She smiled at Kelly.

Kelly felt excited about coaching the Twinklers. Sure, it would be extra work, and lately she seemed to run around nonstop all the time. But it would be fun—the Twinklers always looked so adorable in their tiny leotards. And it would be good experience, too. Someday, when her Olympic career was over, she would need to do something else. Kelly had always thought she'd like to coach, since it would keep her in the world of gymnastics. This would be a great start. Only one thing was bothering her.

"What about Maya?" she asked. "She's just as good as I am. I don't want her to feel left out." Only three months before, there had been no one Kelly's age at SGA who was as good as she was. In fact, in her age group, there hadn't been anyone in the whole state with her talent: She had been last year's regional champion. But her stepsister, Maya, was definitely in her league. At first Kelly had felt threatened by Maya's skill, but now she enjoyed the challenge. Maya's expertise at gymnastics kept Kelly on her toes, and that was fun.

"We've already thought of that, and I think it'll be fine," Emma said. "Maya's decided to take extra academic tutoring on Mondays and Fridays. She's a great student, but I think the language switch is taking its toll. A few weeks of intensive work on her English skills should fix everything up."

"All right, then," Kelly said eagerly. "I'll do it."

"Are you sure? It won't be too much for you on top of everything else?"

"No, I can handle it," Kelly said, jumping out of her seat. "I can't wait."

"Wonderful," Emma said, looking relieved. "You'll be a big help. We can talk more about it tonight at home. And tomorrow you can start with the Twinklers."

"Great!" Kelly hugged her mother quickly, then headed out into the gym to rejoin the Silver Stars. *This time tomorrow I'll be a coach, with my own class,* she thought excitedly. *This is going to be fantastic.*

Chapter Three

Fur, Feather, and Scale was three stores down in the same strip mall as SGA. Monica couldn't get there fast enough. She ran down the sidewalk, the kitten clutched against her chest. Ever since she was a little girl she had had a soft spot in her heart for animals—all animals. But because both her parents were allergic to animal dander, Monica had never been able to get a furry pet. Luckily, Monica's best friend (before Monica had moved to Atlanta) had had two cats, two dogs, a rabbit, some fish, and a large box turtle. Monica had loved going to her house.

Pulling open the door of Fur, Feather, and Scale, Monica went in and headed for the desk. The place smelled faintly of new paint and dog.

"May I help you?" The receptionist was a young woman with golden-blond hair and warm brown eyes. Her name tag read JOLAYNE.

Quickly Monica explained how she had found the kitten at SGA, and uncupped her hands to show it.

"Goodness," Jolayne said sympathetically. "I know Dr. Thayer will want to see it. Come into examining room one."

The examining room had a high table, and Monica set the kitten down on it. It huddled in a miserable little ball and meowed anxiously.

"There, there, sweetie," Monica murmured, stroking its dirty fur. "It'll be okay. The vet will fix you all up."

The minutes ticked by as Monica waited. On the walls were large posters showing the life cycle of the flea, and a cat's digestive and reproductive systems. On another wall was a small plaque with a picture of a cat and a quote: " 'Who can believe that there is no soul behind those luminous eyes!'—Theophile Gautier (1811–1872)." There were also cupboards full of various supplies.

The door finally opened and a young African American woman came in. Her hair was pulled into a neat bun, and she wore a doctor's white coat. A stethoscope hung around her neck. Her eyeglasses had a red cord attached so that she couldn't lose them.

"Hello, I'm Dr. Marian Thayer," the woman said, putting down a manila file and holding out her hand for Monica to shake. Monica shook it, feeling very grown-up. Dr. Thayer was tall, almost five inches taller than Monica. Her voice was friendly and pleasant. Then Monica noticed the vet's earrings—they were tiny silver cowboy boots. At home Monica had some small silver cowboy hat earrings. Monica instantly decided she liked Dr. Thayer.

Once again Monica told the story of finding the kitten, including the part about the tennis players grunting and how they had all heard a small meow.

Dr. Thayer laughed. "I used to play quite a bit of tennis myself," she said. "I don't know if I make weird noises or not."

Smiling, Monica stroked the kitten between its small ears. Her face sobered. "Can you help it? It seems so sick."

"Let's take a look," the vet said calmly. Gently she felt the kitten all over, along its ribs and tiny legs. She listened to its chest with her stethoscope. She took its temperature.

The whole time, Monica waited. Back at SGA, class would be going on. Guiltily, Monica again felt relieved that she wasn't there. She'd probably only be messing up on her vaulting mount, or falling off the beam, or landing too soon on an aerial walkover. Lately it seemed that all her gymnastic talent could fit into her pinkie finger. She sighed.

"How long have you been open?" she asked. "There used to be a needlepoint shop here."

"Only two weeks," Dr. Thayer replied, feeling the kitten again along its skinny stomach. "I used to be a partner in another practice, but then I moved to Atlanta and branched out on my own." She looked at Monica. "Good news," she said, stroking the kitten from head to tail. "He's beat up—he's a he, by the way—hungry, dehydrated, and has both fleas and ear mites."

"That's *good* news?" Monica squealed in horror. Her hands closed protectively around the kitten again.

"And worms," the doctor said. She hung her stethoscope around her neck and smiled at Monica. "The good news is that's all fixable stuff—he'll make it, and he should be fine. No broken bones, no serious illness or wounds. He's just had a hard time, haven't you, boy?" She scratched him absently behind his tiny, pointed ears. The kitten closed his eyes.

"So I suggest we feed him," Dr. Thayer continued, "give him water, bathe him, and get rid of his ear mites and worms. Then he should be as good as new."

Monica had a sudden bad thought. "Um," she began hesitantly. "He's uh, just a stray . . . all that sounds like it's going to cost a lot." She had some money saved up at home, but would it be enough?

Dr. Thayer brushed her worries away. "Don't concern yourself about that," she said. "As part of helping the community, it's my practice to take care of local strays. He seems a sweet young thing. I bet once he's cleaned up and healthy, we'll have no problem adopting him out." She started to write something on the kitten's file.

"Really?" Monica gave a happy little jump. "That's fabulous! I felt so sorry for him. He's just a baby. Thank you so much."

Dr. Thayer smiled. "No problem. Would you like to come back and see him tomorrow?"

"Could I?"

"Sure," the vet said. "You're welcome anytime."

"Great! I don't have class tomorrow, so I could come after school."

"Do you like gymnastics?" Dr. Thayer asked. "When I pass by the gym it always seems to be bustling with activity."

"Yeah, I do like it," Monica said. "I mean, I love it. I've been at SGA ever since I moved to Atlanta two years ago."

"Oh, you're a transplant, like me," the vet said. "Where are you from?"

"New Orleans," Monica answered, petting the kitten softly.

"You're kidding! High five." Dr. Thayer held her hand up, and Monica swatted it. "I'm from New Orleans too. That's where I was a partner in a practice."

"Really?" Monica beamed. She liked the idea that she and Dr. Thayer had things in common.

"Yes. We'll have to talk about it the next time you come. Right now I have to see a golden retriever with a sore paw." Dr. Thayer smiled and held out her hand again, and Monica shook it happily.

"See you tomorrow," Monica said, floating out the door. Her day had suddenly gone from horrible to fabulous in about three seconds. Meeting Dr. Thayer was a big part of the reason.

Out on the sidewalk Monica glanced at her watch and saw that her Silver Star class would be over. She would just run back, grab her duffel, and meet the others at Gianelli's.

Chapter Four

"I'm getting tired of cherry-nut crunch," Kelly said as she slid into the booth next to Maya. The Silvers had a favorite spot way in the back of Gianelli's. Candace and Harry sat on one side, and Kathryn, Maya, and Kelly were squeezed into the other.

"It's too sweet," her stepsister said, wrinkling her nose. "You should try what I'm having." She held up her double cone of chocolate-mint-chip and orange sherbet.

Kelly groaned. "Just because Harry has converted you to her weird tastes doesn't mean *I'll* eat that combination."

Harry grinned and waved her identical double cone.

"It does look revolting," Kathryn said, taking a sip of her strawberry shake.

"It's killer," Maya said.

"Hey, guys." Monica had just come in, and she dumped her duffel on the floor as she slid onto the seat next to Harry. "The kitten is going to be all right."

"Oh, great," Kelly said. "I'm really glad. You'll have to tell us everything. But first—I have some news myself." She looked at her friends.

"Spill it," Candace said.

Kelly beamed proudly. "Guess who's going to be the new Twinklers coach?"

"Who?" Candace asked.

"Do you mean the coach for the new Twinklers, or the new coach for the old Twinklers?" Kathryn asked.

"Guys!" Kelly whined.

Her friends laughed.

"You mean Emma wants you to coach the Twinklers?" Harry asked. "That's great!"

"Thank you," Kelly said.

"That is great, Kelly," Maya said. "You'll be really good at it."

"Thanks," Kelly repeated, glad that Maya didn't seem at all jealous. "It's just until the exhibition at Fitness Week. After that they're hiring a new full-time coach."

"Still, it'll be an incredible experience," Monica said.

"I bet it'll be fun," said Harry. "The Twinklers are so cute."

"Are you getting paid?" Candace asked.

"Candace! That's none of your business," Kathryn said.

"Actually, we didn't talk about money," Kelly admitted. "But I'd do it for free, just to help out."

"Of course you would," Monica said. "It's going to be a blast—you're so lucky."

"Yeah," Kelly said. "Anyway—tell us about the kitten. You missed the whole second half of class."

"Well, the kitten is a boy, and he has a lot of stuff wrong with him, but it can all be fixed," Monica said. "And Dr. Thayer's going to fix him up for free and then find him a good home. Listen, can any of you guys take him?"

"We can ask Papa," Maya said doubtfully.

"We'll try too," Candace said. "But don't get your hopes up."

"I'll ask my grandmother," Harry put in. She lived with her grandmother, father, and two little brothers. Her mother had died when she was seven, just like Maya's.

"Okay. But everyone try hard. The vet is taking care of the kitten for free," Monica said enthusiastically. "She's a woman, and she's black. And guess what? She's from New Orleans, like me.

She's really tall, too. And we even own matching earrings, almost!"

Kelly smiled. She couldn't remember when she'd last seen Monica this excited. At least excited about something besides Beau Jarrett or shopping.

"That's great, Monica," Kelly said. "And she's going to take care of the kitten?"

"Yeah. Dr. Thayer was so gentle with him. I really trust her."

"I'm glad," Harry said. "It was hard to keep my mind on class after you found him. But hey, guess what?" She smiled at Monica. "I did the vaulting mount! Finally. I'm so short that we had to move the masking tape mark up about five inches." She laughed. "The first couple times I came down from my roundoff right in the middle of the springboard. Wham! Didn't bounce at all."

"But you got it in the end," Monica said. "Good for you."

Something in Monica's voice made Kelly glance up at her. "You'll get it too, next time," Kelly said firmly. "It's just that you've grown lately. You have to get used to your new height. If we move the mark back a little bit—"

"Kelly!" Monica interrupted. "I'm as tall as Emma now. My dad is tall, my mom is tall, and

27

Gene is tall. Let's face it: In another year I won't be able to do gymnastics at all!"

Kelly and the rest of the Silver Stars were startled by Monica's outburst.

"That's not true," Kelly protested. "There are plenty of gymnasts who are taller than you."

"Name one." Monica's brown eyes looked steely. "A female one."

Quickly Kelly began to search her memory. "Um . . ." Most gymnasts *were* shorter than Monica. Some were quite a bit shorter. Kelly herself was at least four inches shorter, and Harry was even shorter than that.

"See?" Monica said, sounding upset.

"Svetlana Khorkina," Kathryn said calmly. She slurped up the last of her shake.

"That's right," Maya said. "I remember. She's Russian, like me. She had the second-highest all-around total in the finals at the 1994 team worlds. And she's five-three. An inch taller than you."

"See?" Kelly mimicked Monica.

"Really?" Monica said.

"Yep," Kathryn replied. "I wouldn't worry about your height, Monica. You're really graceful and limber."

"And really strong," Kelly said. She wanted Monica to feel better about gymnastics. "You look fabulous on the beam."

Monica sighed. "Well, thanks, you guys. I appreciate it."

"Besides, look at it this way," Kelly said. "Growing is a perfect excuse to buy all new clothes." She smiled at her friend.

Monica didn't smile back.

Chapter Five

"Man, that math test was killer," Kelly moaned on Friday afternoon. Maya had already left to meet her new English tutor, and Kelly and Monica were walking the eight blocks from school to SGA.

"Yeah, and I even studied for it," Monica agreed. She, Kelly, and Maya all had sixth-period math together at Sugarloaf Middle School. They were in seventh grade, while Harry, Candace, and Kathryn were in sixth grade.

"The word problems are always the worst," Kelly continued.

"And the formulas." Monica swung her duffel bag at her side.

Usually on a Friday she and Kelly would be running home, ready to start celebrating the weekend. But today Kelly was starting to coach the Twinklers, and Monica was going to visit the kitten—and Dr. Thayer. She had been excited about it all day.

"I feel nervous about coaching," Kelly admitted.

"You'll be fine," Monica said. "And they're so cute—I'm sure they won't give you any trouble."

"Yeah, I guess. I wish you were coming with me."

Monica turned to smile at Kelly and realized all over again that she had to look down at her. Just a year ago they had been almost the exact same height. "You'll do fine," Monica told her. "It'll be just like baby-sitting."

"I've never done any baby-sitting," Kelly said.

"Me neither." Monica laughed. "But it'll be okay, you'll see." Today she wasn't going to let anything get her down. She didn't have gymnastics class, and she was going to see Dr. Thayer. Those two things alone were enough to brighten her whole day.

Soon they arrived in front of SGA. The big sign over the doors said SUGARLOAF GYMNASTIC ACADEMY—EMMA STANTON AND DIMITRI RESNIKOV.

"Good luck," Monica told Kelly. "Remember, you're a Silver Star—they look up to you."

"Yeah, you're right. It'll be easy," Kelly said. She gave Monica a little wave. "See you later. Tell the kitten hello from me."

"Okay."

As Kelly pushed through the double glass doors of the gym and disappeared inside, Monica headed down the strip mall to Fur, Feather, and Scale. Suddenly she was worried. What if something had happened to the kitten during the night? What if he hadn't pulled through? What if Dr. Thayer had been wrong about him?

Her heart in her throat, Monica flung open the glass door and rushed inside. In the waiting room, a panting black cocker spaniel sat at the feet of a middle-aged woman. A young boy held a cat box on his lap. Jolayne, the receptionist, smiled at Monica.

"Hi. You're the girl who was here yesterday, right?" she asked. "With the kitten."

"Right," Monica gasped. "Where is he? Is he okay? Can I see him?"

"Sure, he's fine." Jolayne pointed to a door on the right. "Go through that door and down the hall. The kennel assistant, Ana, will help you find him."

"Thanks."

In the hallway Monica saw a small kitchenette, Dr. Thayer's office, and a small room with a table and chairs. At the end of the hall was another door, and she pushed it open.

She was in the middle of a large room. Against three walls, large animal cages were stacked three high. There was a tall table with a built-in sink and another table to groom animals on. A young Hispanic woman wearing blue surgical scrubs came forward, drying her hands on a paper towel.

"May I help you?" she asked with a smile.

"Yes. I'm Monica Hales. Jolayne said you could help me find the kitten I brought in yesterday," Monica explained.

Ana nodded. "The new kitten. He's right over here." She walked over to one of the middle cages and opened the door. A mew came from the back as she reached in. "Come on, sweetie," Ana said coaxingly. Then she brought out the kitten and showed him to Monica.

Monica shook her head. "No, that isn't him," she said. "My kitten was dark gray all over, and sick . . ."

Ana laughed and cuddled the kitten against her shoulder. "This is him," she said. "I promise. But he's had a bath, and food, and IV fluids all night. Haven't you, little guy?"

The kitten meowed again and craned his head to look at Monica. She stared at him in disbelief, then reached for him. Immediately he curled up against her chest, his small body vibrating with a purr.

"He remembers you," Ana said. "The girl who saved him."

"I sure don't remember him like this," Monica said, looking down at the kitten. He looked up at her and meowed again. Instead of being half shut and crusty, his large eyes were a clear, shining blue. He had beautiful pale gray fur, tabby-striped. Three feet were white, and one was gray. The tip of his tail was white. He was still skinny, but he was clean, fluffy, and much, much happier.

"He's beautiful," Monica said in awe, stroking him gently.

"Yes, he cleaned up well, didn't he?" Ana asked. "He's a sweet little guy, too. Give us a few more days to fatten him up, and I bet no one will be able to resist him."

Especially me, Monica thought sadly, thinking forward to the day when someone—not her—would adopt him. But that was how it was. There was nothing she could do about it. Monica sighed and rubbed her face against the kitten. He closed his eyes and tucked his head under her chin.

"I can tell you're a cat lover," Dr. Thayer said, coming up behind Monica.

Monica turned and smiled at the vet. "He looks wonderful! You worked miracles!"

Dr. Thayer laughed. "Not really. Just took care of him the way he ought to be taken care of. You must know a lot about cats."

"Why do you say that?" Monica asked.

"The way you handle him," the vet replied. "You're holding him the right way, and petting him where he likes it."

Monica beamed. "Actually, I don't know a lot about cats—or dogs," she admitted. "But I love all animals. I've always wanted a pet of my own, but I can't have one."

"That's too bad," Dr. Thayer said. "You seem like an animal person. You're gentle and caring, and those are the most important qualities."

Inside, Monica felt as if a warm beam of sunlight were filling her chest. Dr. Thayer was so nice. It felt good to be complimented. Monica gestured to the cages lining the walls. "What are these animals here for?"

"Well, let's see," Dr. Thayer said, walking over to one bank of animal pens. She pointed to a small dog asleep on a chewed-up section of quilt. "That's Toby. He was neutered this morning, and he's sleeping off the anesthetic. His owner brought in his favorite quilt so he wouldn't feel so alone."

Next she reached through the bars and stroked the nose of a huge orange cat that was pushing his head against the door. "This is Whiskers. His owners are away for the weekend, so he's staying with us."

Down the line she went. She knew every animal by name and had something nice to say to each of them. Some were there for surgery or treatment, and some were being boarded. Besides Monica's kitten, there were two other strays waiting to be adopted. They were older and somewhat less cute, Monica decided. But all the animals were eager to see Dr. Thayer and came forward in their pens to be petted and talked to.

"Some of them look lonely," Monica said hesitantly.

"Yes," Dr. Thayer agreed. "We try to play with them, but we have other duties too. It's hard to give each one as much attention as we'd like. And I can't afford to hire another full-time assistant. Maybe in several months . . ."

Monica wished she could help out somehow. It would be so cool to have a job like Ana's, where she took care of pets all day.

Just then Dr. Thayer glanced at her watch. "I'd better get back," she said. "I have a sick parrot coming in soon, and I have to review his file."

"A sick parrot!" Monica exclaimed. "What's wrong with him?"

Dr. Thayer laughed. "He has laryngitis! I bet he has a cold—or maybe he's been talking too much."

Monica and Ana joined in the laughter.

"Do you see other unusual pets?" Monica asked.

Dr. Thayer nodded. "Of course. At veterinary school we have to learn about all kinds of animals—including farm animals, some zoo animals, and all sorts of what they call exotics. It's pretty normal for me to see rabbits, ferrets, birds, snakes, turtles . . . even raccoons and opossums sometimes."

"Wow!" Monica's mind was racing. Dr. Thayer's life sounded incredibly exciting. Every day brought something new. Gymnastics had a lot of repetition in it; you had to work on a move over and over until it was perfect. Here, you never knew what was waiting for you. *And best of all, it doesn't matter how tall you are,* Monica thought.

"I'd better go," said the vet. "Thanks for stopping by. Please come back anytime."

"Thanks." Monica smiled good-bye at Dr. Thayer, then regretfully put her kitten back in his pen. He mewed and scrambled to chase a catnip mouse that was lurking under his faded towel. "I'll come see you again soon," Monica whispered. "That's a promise."

Chapter Six

"Okay, Twinklers!" Kelly clapped her hands twice, the way Emma and Dimitri did. For the past twenty minutes, Kelly had been assisting while Emma put the Twinklers through their paces. Now, for the last half of class, Kelly was on her own. She swallowed, hoping she didn't look half as nervous as she felt. In her navy blue leggings, white T-shirt, and navy blue SGA warm-up jacket with the logo embroidered in gold thread, she hoped she looked grown-up and professional.

"Look at that," Randi Marshall said as she walked by with Julie Stiller. They were both Gold Stars and incredible snobs. Kelly couldn't stand them.

"Yeah. It's the blind leading the blind," Julie drawled as she and Randi headed to the uneven parallel bars. They both laughed, and Kelly felt her cheeks burning.

Put them out of your mind, she commanded herself. *You have a job to do. After all, Mom didn't ask one of them to coach the Twinklers.* With that thought, Kelly felt better.

"Okay, Twinklers," she repeated. "Let's move over to the floor mats, and we'll try some of our somersaults." She clapped again, and the little kids, pushing and giggling, trooped to the floor mats next to the windows.

There were six Twinklers, and they were all either four or five years old. There were no boys. Kelly thought they were adorable—they still had little-girl bodies, with rounded tummies, arms, and legs. In another few years they would take on the leaner, more muscled look of the older gymnast. If they stuck with it, that is.

"Everyone line up, please, single file," Kelly said, pointing to where she wanted the line to begin. "Now, one at a time, I want you to do somersaults across the mats. Be sure to make each movement crisp and smooth. The next person in line can start when the first person has crossed the red line on the mat." Kelly showed them exactly where. "Okay, now, begin, Isabel."

A pretty little girl in a pale pink leotard took her fingers out of her mouth, walked to the edge of the mats, knelt down, and did a somersault. She stood up and grinned at Kelly, and Kelly grinned back.

"Very good, Isabel," Kelly said encouragingly. "Can you do some more for me?"

Kelly was trying to remember what her mother had said to her, back when she was a Twinkler. There had been another woman coach too, and Kelly remembered her as being very kind and encouraging. Now Kelly tried to be the same way.

Isabel nodded solemnly, then knelt down and did more somersaults across the mats.

"Patty, you're next," Kelly said, motioning for Patty to go.

Patty, who had thick brown hair in two braids down to her waist, did her somersaults. Some of them were pretty wobbly, and once she rolled right off the edge of the mat, but Kelly congratulated her all the same.

Calmly and patiently Kelly led the other four through their somersaults, once getting down beside Tania and helping her tuck her head.

Tania rolled.

"There you go!" Kelly praised her. "Very good."

Tania beamed.

"Okay," Kelly said, clapping twice. "Now let's do some cartwheels. I know you can all do cartwheels." She felt happy and proud. Her mother and Dimitri would be pleased to see how well she was coaching this class. It was turning out to be much easier than she had feared.

40

The Twinklers lined up again and began to do cartwheels down the mats.

Their cartwheels were less successful than their somersaults, but Isabel, Maria, and Leeza did them all correctly. Patty, Tania, and Ginger needed more help. Kelly spotted them while they repeated their cartwheels. Putting one hand on their stomachs and one on their backs, she tried to help them stay straight up and down as they turned.

"Good, Patty," she said. "Now just keep your arms and legs as straight as possible."

"They *have* to bend a little," Patty said.

"Well, yes, maybe just a tiny bit," Kelly said, surprised that Patty was disagreeing with her. When she was little she had never questioned her coaches. "But in general they have to keep pretty straight for the cartwheel to work."

Patty tried again, and Kelly decided that was enough cartwheels for today.

"Now we'll try something new," she said. "The back walkover." She felt excited that she would be teaching them a completely new skill. Years from now they would remember her as the coach who taught them the back walkover. The night before, she and Emma had discussed the best way to teach the Twinklers this new skill.

"The back walkover is very easy," Kelly said. "We'll learn it in parts, then put the parts together. First we'll make bridges, on the ground. Once you all make a nice bridge, we'll go on to step two."

Kelly took off her warm-up jacket and lay on her back on the floor mats. She bent her knees so that her feet were flat on the ground, and put her hands up on either side of her head, by her shoulders. Pushing with her arms and legs, she made a bridge, arching her back and letting her head hang down. Then, slowly, so that the Twinklers could see, she pushed off with one foot, then the other, until she was holding herself up in a handstand. When her feet touched the ground on the other side, she pushed off with her hands and stood up, facing the same direction she had started in.

"There. See? It's pretty easy," she told the Twinklers. "But we'll take it slow and start with just bridges. Now, everyone on her back."

The Twinklers dropped excitedly to the floor. Isabel quickly put her hands and legs in the right position and pushed up.

"Perfect, Isabel," Kelly said. Isabel smiled, then lowered herself to the mat. She pushed up a couple of more times into her bridge.

"That's great, Isabel. And Leeza, you have it too. Terrific," Kelly said. When she looked at the other Twinklers, though, her first thought was that

42

a bunch of small, plump fish had been dumped on a dock and were now gasping for air. Tania, Patty, Maria, and Ginger were trying to make bridges but were mostly just flopping around.

Tania's hands were in the wrong place. Patty's legs were too straight. Maria could get up but couldn't hold the position. Ginger got up but tilted sideways and fell with a crash onto the mats. Kelly had never seen anyone do that before.

"Okay, kids, okay!" Kelly clapped twice. "Let's take it one step at a time. Tania, you begin. I'll spot you."

Tania lay down, and Kelly helped put her feet and hands in the correct positions.

"Now push up," Kelly instructed, placing one hand under Tania's back and lifting. "Good. Everyone, see how she's doing this?" Glancing at the other Twinklers to make sure they understood, Kelly saw that Maria had gotten herself into a shaky handstand and seemed too scared to get down.

"Hang on, Maria," Kelly said, quickly leaving Tania and rushing over to her. Just as she was helping the little girl lower herself to the mat, Tania's bridge collapsed.

At the same time, Patty successfully pushed herself into a bridge, while Ginger started her walkover from a standing position, which she wasn't ready to try. The Twinklers were getting a little out of control.

"Good, Patty," Kelly said, heading over to them. "Ginger, wait a second—"

Suddenly Ginger screamed and leaped forward, her eyes wide. She didn't look where she was going and crashed into Patty, collapsing her bridge and splatting down on top of her.

Patty's face crumpled, her mouth opened, and a huge wail hit Kelly's ears.

"Owwwwowwowww!"

Rushing over, Kelly pushed Ginger off Patty and gathered Patty in her arms. "Are you okay? I'm sure you're okay. Now, now, you were just surprised, right?" Kelly babbled, trying to soothe the little girl. Patty sniffled and nodded.

"Ginger, what's the matter with you?" Kelly asked, trying to keep calm. "Why did you yell?"

"I saw a mouse!" Ginger exclaimed, pointing at the floor under the window.

Instantly all the Twinklers and Kelly stared over at the wall. Kelly didn't see anything.

"I don't think we have mice," Kelly said firmly, "and I sure don't want to see one. Now, why don't we—" But just as she stood up, Ginger did another cartwheel right on top of Isabel. Outraged, Isabel smacked Ginger on the bottom. As Kelly watched in horror, Ginger whirled and pushed Isabel as hard as she could, knocking her down on top of Tania and Maria, who collapsed with angry squeals.

They immediately popped up and started to chase Ginger, who ran behind Kelly and clutched her legs. The perfect class was becoming a disaster class. Kelly began to panic. What if her mother or Dimitri or Susan Lu saw this mess? What if the Gold Stars did? She had to regain control—fast!

"All right!" Kelly yelled, clapping her hands hard. She reached out and grabbed Tania and Maria, halting them in their tracks. "Look, everyone just knock it off!" She pushed on Tania's and Maria's shoulders until they sat down with two little plops.

Then she grabbed Ginger, hauled her in front, and sat her down hard next to them. She pointed a stern finger at Leeza, Isabel, and Patty. "You guys sit here. Now, everyone be quiet and don't move a muscle until I say to!" She glared at them all fiercely.

Taking a deep breath, she stepped back and examined the situation. Fortunately, her mother seemed to be in her office, and Dimitri and Susan had the Gold Stars so occupied that they hadn't noticed anything. Kelly turned quickly back to her students.

The six Twinklers were sitting in a miserable,

45

huddled row. Several of them were sniffling; they all looked depressed.

"She's mean," Kelly heard Tania whisper to Maria. Maria nodded as Kelly's cheeks burned with embarrassment. She hadn't meant to be mean. It had just happened. Now she glanced at the clock and saw with relief that it was time for the class to end. Emma came over and smiled. If she was surprised to see the Twinklers looking so unhappy, she didn't show it.

"Okay, girls," Emma said gently. "You may go get changed now. I'll see you again on Monday."

Suddenly looking happy again, the six little girls bounced up and tore off toward the locker room, as if they'd never been so glad to have a class end.

"Rough afternoon, huh?" Emma asked as she put her arm around Kelly's shoulder.

"Oh, Mom," Kelly wailed. "I did everything wrong. I tried so hard to be a good coach, but I couldn't control them, and I yelled, and they fought . . . and Ginger said she saw a mouse."

Emma frowned. "A mouse? That's strange. Dimitri said it looked as if one of our mats had been chewed on by a mouse. I hope we don't have a problem. I'd hate to have to call in an exterminator. Anyway," she continued soothingly, "it was only your first day, honey. You can't be perfect straight off. It's like everything else in gymnastics: You have to work at it. With more practice, I'm sure you'll be a better coach."

Kelly sighed. "I sure hope so—for their sakes!"

Chapter Seven

"The bad thing about Sundays is that you know Monday is just around the corner," Kelly sighed. "Monday, and the Twinklers." She was curled up in the hammock on the upstairs front porch. A new *Young Gymnast* magazine lay open next to her.

"Yes," Maya agreed from where she was stretched out on the porch swing. Kelly had told Maya about the whole Twinkler disaster on Friday.

"Say 'yeah,' Maya, not 'yes,'" Kelly instructed. "You speak too properly all the time." Kelly knew that this was because Maya had learned English as a second language and didn't know all the slang.

"Yeah," Maya said, practicing.

"Good. By the way, how's tutoring going?"

Maya blushed.

"Why are you turning beet red?" Kelly asked curiously. Her eyes narrowed. "Who's your tutor, anyway?"

Groaning, Maya put her latest Casey Montana mystery over her face.

"Come on, spill it," Kelly demanded. After almost three months of living together, she and her stepsister were comfortable with each other. It helped that they both loved gymnastics and went to the same school—that gave them a couple of big things in common. Besides their parents, that is. But it was also nice that they had different friends. Monica was still Kelly's best friend, and Maya liked to hang out with Harry.

Still, as time passed, Kelly was feeling more and more as if she and Maya were truly related, truly part of the same family. It was a nice feeling.

"It's Michael Ashton," Maya said in a muffled voice.

"Who's that?"

Maya took the book off her face and sat up. "Michael Ashton," she repeated. "He's a ninth-grader at Sugarloaf High."

"Uh-huh," Kelly said patiently. "So he's a fourteen-year-old egghead. Why are you acting so weird?"

"He's a really cute egghead," Maya said.

Kelly's eyes glittered. "He's cute?"

Maya nodded. "He's *really* cute. I mean, he's too old—and I don't have time for boys anyway. Gymnastics is much more important. But Michael is nice. He's very patient, and funny. It makes it hard to concentrate sometimes."

Laughing, Kelly leaned back in the hammock. "Well, I hope you're bringing up your English grade," she said. "Or Mom and Dimitri will have wasted their money."

"I *am* working on it," Maya said. "I'm not just goofing off."

Inside the house, they heard Dimitri say, "Hold this, please, dear."

Maya groaned softly and clapped a hand to her forehead. "What now?"

"It's that bookcase he made," Kelly explained. Lately Dimitri was on a handyman kick. He kept trying to fix things around the big Victorian house they had all moved into after he and Emma got married. Unfortunately, he usually just made things worse. After he'd tried to fix the sink in the girls' bathroom, they'd had to brush their teeth in the kitchen for almost two weeks, until Emma finally called a plumber.

"They're wiring the bookcase to the wall in the hallway, so it can't tip over," Kelly said.

Maya sighed and rolled her eyes. "Anyway, are you worried about tomorrow afternoon?"

"Ugh—don't remind me," Kelly said.

"It'll go a lot better this time," Maya predicted. "Now you know what to expect and what you need to do. Tomorrow will be more fun. You'll see. I wish I could coach sometime."

"Yeah, well, I won't rush to say yes next time Mom asks me," Kelly said.

"Are you going to see Monica later?" Maya asked. Monica lived only about four blocks away from Kelly and Maya.

Kelly shook her head. "I think she mentioned she was going back to the vet's."

"Again?" Maya's blond eyebrows went up. "She was there just yesterday when we all went."

The day before, after the Silvers had finished their usual Saturday-morning class, Monica had asked if they wanted to see the kitten she and Kelly had rescued. Of course they all did, so they had trooped down to Fur, Feather, and Scale.

"I couldn't get over how great he looked," Kelly said. "He's really pretty."

"Yeah," Maya agreed, remembering not to say "Yes." She added, "The vet did a good job on him. She was really nice. I can see why Monica has been going there lately."

"I wish we could take the kitten," Kelly said. She and Maya had asked their parents, but because they had such hectic schedules, they had decided their home wouldn't be best for the cat.

"I like cats," Maya said. "My grandmother had

51

a cat." For just a moment, a sad expression crossed her face. When Maya and Dimitri had moved to America so that Dimitri could marry Emma, Maya had left her grandmother behind. Kelly knew she missed her very much, even though they wrote back and forth and talked on the phone sometimes.

"But Monica *has* been there a lot in her spare time," Kelly said. "I mean, yesterday she didn't even want to go to Gianelli's with us. She just wanted to hang out and play with all the animals."

"Maybe she feels sad that she can't have a pet," Maya suggested. "And going to the vet's is the next-best thing."

"Maybe," Kelly said, thinking that Monica had another reason—a reason to do with gymnastics. "Are you looking forward to Fitness Week?"

Maya nodded. "It will be great if we can get more people interested in gymnastics."

"I just like performing in public," Kelly admitted with a grin. "It's good practice for when we have to perform in the World Championships, or even the Olympics."

"True," Maya said, sitting up. She held up her hand, and she and Kelly slapped high five.

Crash!

Maya jumped out of the swing, startled. "What was that?"

Kelly rolled out of the hammock, pulled open the screen door, and raced inside. Maya was right behind her. Down the hall, Kelly could see Dimitri and Emma standing with surprised expressions. The bookcase was in pieces on the floor, and a big cloud of dust was settling on everything. Kelly looked at the wall. Large chunks of plaster had fallen off and were now lying around the bookcase.

"Oh, Papa," Maya breathed, then sneezed because of the dust.

"These walls are too old to support any weight, I guess," Emma said.

Kelly saw Dimitri's disappointment and felt sorry for him. He really enjoyed his handyman projects, even if no one else did.

"It's okay, Dimitri," Kelly said. "You can put your bookcase back together. But first," she added, "you need to fix the plaster on the wall." She took a deep breath. "Good thing you're so handy." She could tell what was coming: buckets of plaster being mixed in the kitchen, Dimitri getting plaster everywhere, the wall looking uneven and patchy . . .

But she knew she had said the right thing.

Dimitri's look of disappointment eased, and he gazed at the wall with interest. He leaned over and tapped against the holes with his fingers.

"Yes," he said thoughtfully. "I will need to get some plaster mix. . . ."

Emma, Kelly, and Maya all looked at each other at the same time and smothered their laughter.

———

"There you go, little guy," Monica said, tossing a catnip mouse across the floor. Her abandoned kitten raced after it, then subdued it with a ferocious pounce.

Since it was Sunday afternoon, Dr. Thayer wasn't at Fur, Feather, and Scale. Only Ana, the kennel assistant, was. Monica was helping her clean the animal pens. Or rather, Monica was playing with each animal while Ana cleaned its pen.

Ana looked down at her and laughed. "You must have emptied the pet-supply store," she said.

Monica tossed the catnip mouse again and shrugged. This morning she had shown up with a bag full of cat and dog toys that she had bought herself. She'd made sure each animal in the kennels had at least one toy.

"It's the least I can do," Monica said. "Dr. Thayer won't let me give her any money to take care of Sam Gordon Andrew."

The kitten stood up on his hind legs and batted the mouse in the air.

"Oh, so you've named him, then?" Ana asked. She leaned into a cage and spritzed the floor and walls with disinfectant.

"Yes," Monica said. "I know his new owners will rename him, but in the meantime I'm going to call him that. You know, Sam Gordon Andrew, because we found him at *SGA*."

"It's a nice name," Ana said. She put a clean, soft towel into the pen, then a fresh metal pan of kitty litter. "Okay, fella. All fresh and clean."

"I'll play with you again later," Monica promised Sam Gordon Andrew as she lifted him into his cage. She tossed the catnip mouse in with him, and he attacked it again.

The next pen belonged to a small dachshund that was being treated for an ear infection. Ana put him on the grooming table and clipped the lead to his collar. While she cleaned his pen, Monica brushed him all over. He seemed to enjoy it.

"It's so peaceful here," Monica said. She thought of how it was at SGA—always brightly lit, with tons of people working, practicing, talking, shouting. Always lots of action and excitement. It used to seem exhilarating to Monica, but now thinking about it made her neck muscles tense up.

"Not always," Ana said. "Last week we had three emergencies in the same day. We were running around like crazy. And then Jimmy Tadwell's ferret got loose in the waiting room, and Mrs. Carlisle's Doberman went bonkers trying to get it." Ana chuckled. "But that was pretty unusual."

Smiling, Monica brushed the little dachshund one last time from his nose to the tip of his wagging tail. "Still," she said, "it's just so nice being here, taking care of the animals."

"Well, we're glad to have you around," Ana said. She put the now shiny dachshund back in his pen and took out a large black cat. "You're making a real difference with these guys."

"I am?" Monica felt a warm glow inside. She took Cinders and put him on the table for his brushing.

"Definitely," Ana said. "They're glad to see you, and their owners have noticed that they look extra-spiffy lately. Your being here, caring about them, helps them get better sooner. They love you—and you have such a good way with them."

"Thanks," Monica said, feeling shy and pleased. "I wish I could come more often." She frowned. It would be heaven to come here every afternoon, and see all the animals, and talk to Dr. Thayer, and hang out with Jolayne and Ana. But she couldn't. Her commitment to being in the Silver Stars took a lot of time—especially with the Fitness Week exhibition coming up. *I wish I could skip this one show,* she thought, brushing Cinders's fur gently. *Then I would have so much more time here, where I'm happy.*

Chapter Eight

Kelly put one leg on the barre in front of the mirrored wall at SGA. With her toes pointed, she slowly leaned over and touched her forehead to her knee. In the mirror she saw that her brown hair was already coming out of its bun. Today she was wearing a new leotard. It was sleeveless and coral pink, a real improvement over her usual worn and faded ones.

Next to her, Maya was also stretching.

"I'm so glad today is Tuesday," Kelly said. "I don't have to think about the Twinklers for three whole days."

Maya met Kelly's eyes in the mirror. "Yeah, it sounds like you had another hard time yesterday."

Kelly grimaced at the memory. Yesterday's class had been even worse than Friday's. One Twinkler had called in and said she was sick, which Kelly suspected wasn't true. The others had been first wary and subdued, then rambunctious and loud. When Kelly tried to overlook their behavior, they ran all over her. When she yelled at them or made them sit down, they got angry and weepy. She couldn't win.

But now she was back to being Kelly Reynolds, Silver Star. It felt great.

"Where's Monica?" Kathryn asked. She stood near Kelly and Maya, doing practice handstands.

Kelly glanced around. "I don't know. I figured she was probably still changing. She was at school today, and she didn't mention not coming to class."

"It's weird for her to be late," Harry said, stretching her arms overhead. "Now, if it was Candace . . ."

"Very funny," Candace growled, but she smiled. Everyone knew promptness was not her strong point. "You know I've been on time almost every day lately."

"That's true," her twin, Kathryn, said. She frowned. "Where's the real Candace, and what have you done with her?"

Kelly and Maya snickered.

"Okay, Silvers!" Emma called. "Everybody over here at the vault. I want to go through some moves for Fitness Week."

Kelly looked for Monica one last time. Monica was never late. During sixth-period math, Monica hadn't said anything that made Kelly think she'd be late or wouldn't come to class. *I hope nothing's happened to her,* Kelly thought. What if she'd had an accident on her bike, or what if . . .

"Hi, everyone!" Monica panted as she raced through the gym. "Sorry I'm late, Emma. I'll change real fast!" She burst through the locker room door and was back again in two minutes, wearing a heather-gray unitard. Quickly she gathered her puffy ringlets into a ponytail and snapped a scrunchie into place.

As Emma went over the simple routine they would perform on the vault for Fitness Week, Monica warmed up.

"Each Silver will perform two vaults," Emma explained. "You may choose which two from this list of five. During the exhibition, I want you to move quickly and smoothly. When you land after your vault, do a quick 'touchdown.' " She raised her arms overhead in the traditional position. "Then get out of the way fast, because another gymnast is going to be right behind you. Now look at this list for a minute and choose your two vaults. Choose moves that you do well and are comfortable with. This exhibition isn't a time to show off new moves or stretch your abilities."

Emma carried the list around. When she reached Monica, she patted Monica's shoulder. "Everything okay, honey?" she asked. "Did you have a problem after school?"

To Kelly's surprise, Monica blushed. "No, Emma," she mumbled. "I'm sorry I was late."

Emma smiled and shrugged. "Everyone line up here. Pretend you're at Fitness Week. Run, take your vault, get out the way, and get back in line. We'll make the circuit twice. When everyone has done two vaults, stand neatly at attention by the side of the mats. This is a trial run. Harry, you start."

Harry trotted down to the end of the mats and took a moment to concentrate.

"What happened?" Kelly whispered to Monica as they waited their turns. "I was worried."

"Sorry," Monica whispered back. "I just stopped in at Dr. Thayer's for a second. I guess I lost track of time."

Harry ran down the mats, did a simple straddle vault, and landed perfectly. Then she quickly jumped to the side so that Candace could follow her.

The other Silvers shuffled forward in line.

Kelly wasn't watching. She couldn't believe Monica had been late to SGA because she had gone to the vet's.

Candace did a clean somersault vault, and Maya went to the starting line.

Kelly took a few more steps forward. She was confused and alarmed by what Monica had said. She felt sorry for the kitten too, but still . . .

Maya did a squat vault; Kathryn did a straddle vault, like Harry; and Kelly decided to do a somersault.

After a perfect landing, Kelly quickly got out of the way so that Monica could go.

She watched as her friend ran down the long line of mats, pumping her arms. Monica's ponytail bounced as she popped off the springboard and reached for the vault. When she tucked her knees, Kelly saw that Monica was doing a squat vault. But something went wrong.

Somehow Monica didn't curl her legs up tightly enough, and her toes dragged across the top of the vault. This prevented her from getting enough power to fly forward and make her landing on the crash mat beyond the horse. Her vault self-destructed in front of everyone. Monica never uncurled, and she slid in an awkward mess to the mat next to the vault.

"Monica!" Kelly ran forward as Monica began to sit up. "Are you okay?"

"No," Monica said tightly.

"Did you hurt something?" Emma asked. She

helped Monica stand up and brushed her off. "You know, I think it's those long legs of yours," Emma said cheerfully as she checked Monica for damage. "You're still not used to having to tuck really tight. But don't worry—your skills will catch up to your body soon, and it'll all feel natural again." She smiled and smoothed Monica's hair.

"Yeah, sure," Monica said. "Whatever you say." She let out a long, controlled breath and walked over to the water fountain.

Kelly hurried after her. "Monica, what's wrong? You didn't land that hard, did you?"

Monica sighed and wiped her mouth. "I'm okay. Just leave me alone, all right, Kelly?" Her head hanging, Monica walked slowly back to the group of Silvers ready to go for their second vaults.

"Whatever you say," Kelly said hesitantly. She was going to have to talk to Monica. Something was bothering her best friend, and Kelly intended to find out what.

———————

"Geez, it's really hot out," Kelly said, swinging her backpack from side to side. "Only a few more weeks till the Olympics. I can't wait. Mom and Dimitri managed to get tickets to the gymnastics events."

"Great," Monica answered. She could sense that her best friend had a hidden agenda behind her innocent chatter. Anyway, at least Tuesday's class was over. Now she, Kelly, and Maya were walking home. Since they lived so close, they often walked home together.

"What's for dinner?" Maya asked Kelly.

"Baked potatoes with cheddar, broccoli, and bacon," Kelly answered. "Wanna help me grate the cheese?"

"Sure. As long as you're not going to make your scrambled egg thing."

Laughing, Kelly swatted her stepsister. "It wasn't so bad, and you know it! Remember your pickled cabbage delight."

"Oh, everyone likes pickled cabbage," Maya insisted with a grin. "You're just weird, that's all."

Monica glumly regarded her friends as they teased each other. She was glad that they got along now, but today it made her feel like an outsider. Kelly and Maya lived together—they were making all sorts of memories together. And they had a huge thing in common: They both loved gymnastics more than anything. Just three weeks ago, Monica would have felt the same and felt just as much a part of the Silvers. But now she didn't know.

"Earth to Monica," Kelly was saying. "Come

in, Monica." She pretended to hit a communication badge on her chest.

"Oh, sorry," Monica said, shaking her head. She made herself smile.

"What's the matter, Monica?" Kelly asked softly. "You were late to class today, and then . . ."

"And then I totally messed up and made a fool of myself?" Monica finished for her. "I know."

"That's not what I was going to say," Kelly protested.

"Well, it's no big deal," Monica said. "I just stopped by the vet's to see Sam Gordon Andrew, and I lost track of time."

"Sam Gordon Andrew?" Maya asked.

"The kitten. For SGA," Monica explained. "He's doing great." She brightened, remembering how his little body was plumping up, how his fur was getting thicker and shinier. "I love him a lot," she added, suddenly feeling down again. "I know he's going to be adopted soon."

Monica's Birkenstocks scuffed along the sidewalk.

"You really like going to the vet's," Maya said, brushing her long blond hair back.

"Yeah," Monica said. "It's so interesting. Just yesterday I helped Dr. Thayer with a dog that has diabetes. He's doing fine, but he needs insulin injections, just like a human. Oh, and then a rabbit got out of his cage somehow! We were all chasing him up and down the halls. . . ." Monica laughed, thinking about it. "Finally I took off my sweatshirt and threw it over him, and Ana grabbed him." Ana had complimented her on her quick thinking, Monica remembered with a warm glow. At Fur, Feather, and Scale, Monica seemed to do everything right. At SGA lately, it seemed as if she did nothing right.

Monica sighed.

"It's really great that you like going there so much," Kelly told her. "And I bet they like having you. But I'm worried that it might get in the way of what's really important—gymnastics."

Monica looked down at Kelly and saw the concern in her friend's eyes. She remembered when they had been the same height. "Is gymnastics what's really important, Kel?" she asked, suddenly feeling as if all her emotions were going to pour out of her. "I mean, I can't even do a simple squat vault. I'm off balance on the beam, I almost killed myself on the uneven parallel bars last week, and . . . I don't know. I used to be good at gymnastics, but not anymore."

"Oh, Monica," Kelly began. "You just have to—"

"But at Dr. Thayer's," Monica interrupted, "I do everything right. It isn't difficult. And it doesn't

66

take hours and days and weeks of practice. I don't pull muscles or land badly or work so hard that my arms shake. And I really admire Dr. Thayer. It makes me think I can do anything and be good at it."

Kelly gazed at Monica earnestly. "You *can* do anything. You're already good at gymnastics, Monica, and if—"

"Kelly, I'm not. Don't you see? I *used* to be good at gymnastics, but not anymore. And I might never be again. Maybe I should try to be good at something else."

Kelly's eyes widened. She looked at Maya for help, then back at Monica. "Something else? What are you saying?"

"Are you quitting SGA?" Maya asked.

"No, no—I'm not," Monica said quickly, sorry that she had upset Kelly. "It's just frustrating to not be able to do things that used to be a snap, that's all. And I wish I didn't have to worry about this Fitness Week exhibition. But it'll probably all blow over. Don't . . . don't worry about it. I don't even know why I'm saying this stuff."

Looking doubtful, Kelly started walking again. Monica could see the hurt on her face. This time *she* looked at Maya for help, but Maya's tentative smile offered her little comfort.

They walked on in silence.

Chapter Nine

Well, maybe just for one minute, Monica thought, pushing through the doors at Fur, Feather, and Scale on Wednesday afternoon. *If I stay only a minute, I won't be late to SGA.*

After a lot of thinking the night before, Monica had decided that she couldn't give up gymnastics without a fight. She had vowed to work extra-hard at it until she felt comfortable with all her old skills. After all, gymnastics had made her happy since she was eight years old—before her family had moved to Atlanta. Before she had met Kelly. Gymnastics deserved another chance.

And yet here she was at Dr. Thayer's, smiling across the reception desk at Jolayne. Jolayne was on the phone but waved Monica through the doors to the kennel room in back.

A quick glance at her watch showed Monica that she had exactly three minutes before she was due at SGA. Four minutes, or even five, if she skimped a tiny bit on warming up.

In the kennel room, Ana was clipping long, matted hair off an English sheepdog.

"Hi, Monica," she said cheerfully. Her electric razor moved smoothly and surely over the animal's thick coat, and huge globs of fur peeled off and fell to the floor.

"Won't he feel naked without his hair?" Monica asked.

"I'm leaving about an inch on. It'll grow back pretty quickly," Ana explained. "Right now his coat is so matted and tangled that it's causing him skin problems. With it nice and short, his owners can get into good habits about his grooming, and hopefully this won't happen again."

The sheepdog thumped his tail against the table and turned his head to pant cheerfully at Monica. He looked a lot smaller without all his hair.

"Hey, boy," Monica said to the dog, patting him. Then she crossed the room to the kitten's cage and peered inside. Sam Gordon Andrew was there, curled up asleep on his old towel. One of the catnip toys that Monica had brought him was lying by his side. He looked so adorable that a lump formed in Monica's throat. If only she could keep him . . .

"Hi there, Ms. Hales."

69

Monica turned to see Dr. Thayer smiling at her.

"Hi, Dr. Thayer," Monica said. "I haven't seen you in a while."

The vet nodded. "I've been crazy busy," she said. "But Ana and Jolayne have told me about how great you've been with our guests." She waved a hand at the animal pens. "I really appreciate it. You're a very giving person."

Monica felt a familiar warm glow washing over her. It was the feeling she always got when she was at Fur, Feather, and Scale.

"Can I ask you for a favor?" Dr. Thayer said.

"Anything," Monica said eagerly.

"Well, Ana is busy with Herman, here," Dr. Thayer said, pointing at the sheepdog. "So could you lend me a hand in examining room one? I have a cat that needs a shot."

"Me!" Monica exclaimed.

Dr. Thayer grinned. "You. I'll tell you exactly what to do, okay?"

Dropping her duffel by the door, Monica followed the vet into the examining room. It was the first time she would help a patient while the owner was there.

Now she saw a nervous-looking young man cradling a large Siamese cat in his arms. The cat was growling threateningly.

"Hush, Caesar," the man crooned softly. "Hush, boy."

"Mr. Ortiz, this is my assistant, Monica," Dr. Thayer said confidently. "She's going to help hold Caesar while I give him his rabies booster."

Monica straightened up as tall as she could and beamed with pride. She tried to look like a professional vet's assistant.

"Here, Monica." Dr. Thayer held out some heavy suede gloves that came past her elbows. Monica put them on and rubbed her hands together experimentally. She could hardly feel a thing.

The vet gently pulled Caesar away from his owner and put him on the table. Caesar huddled there, looking miserable and growling from deep in his throat.

"He won't bite," Mr. Ortiz assured them. "He's never scratched or bitten anyone."

"Hold him very firmly here at the scruff of his neck," Dr. Thayer instructed Monica. "And here, at his hips. Then, when I start to give the injection, jiggle his head just a tiny bit. It will distract him."

Monica tried not to show how unsure she felt as she gripped the cat exactly where Dr. Thayer had showed her. The cat turned to look at her with large blue eyes, and Monica smiled at him.

"It's okay, boy," she said calmly. "What a pretty cat you are. So big and healthy. Yes, you are. And your daddy loves you."

Mr. Ortiz smiled.

"Now jiggle him," the vet said softly.

Gently Monica wiggled the cat's head for a few seconds, waiting for Dr. Thayer to give him his shot.

"All over!" Dr. Thayer said, disposing of the needle.

"You already did it?" Monica asked. "Caesar didn't react at all."

"That's because you did such a good job holding him," Dr. Thayer said with a smile.

Monica smiled back, then stroked Caesar through her heavy gloves. He relaxed a little and raised his head to be petted.

"He's never been this good at the vet's before," Mr. Ortiz said, getting Caesar's carrying case ready.

"He's never had the magic hands of Monica Hales on him before," Dr. Thayer said, writing something on Caesar's chart.

Monica felt wonderful. "Wait till I tell Kelly about this," she said. "She's my best friend."

"Does she do gymnastics too?" the vet asked.

"Yeah." Monica nodded. "She's incredible. She'll probably be in the next Olympics. I wish you could meet her—you weren't here the day everyone came."

"I'd like to meet her," Dr. Thayer said with a smile.

After Caesar had gone, Monica helped Dr. Thayer with a small pug dog that also needed to be held while he had a shot, and then she helped with a large Dalmatian puppy that needed to have stitches taken out. With the big gloves on, Monica felt safe, and Dr. Thayer always told her exactly what to do. She wasn't frightened or disgusted by any of the procedures. When she mentioned this to the vet, Dr. Thayer gave her a speculative glance.

"Maybe you have an affinity for veterinary work," she said.

Her words sent a shiver down Monica's spine. "You think so?" she breathed.

"Well, you're pretty young yet, so you don't have to decide now," Dr. Thayer said with a laugh. "And besides, you're really into gymnastics. Your main focus is on that, right?"

Gymnastics! With a sickening feeling in the pit of her stomach, Monica glanced fearfully at her watch. Quarter to five! She bit back a groan. Class at SGA was half over! How could she have done this?

"Um, yeah," Monica muttered. "Actually, I

73

better get going. But thanks for letting me help today." Not even the horrible dread could take away how wonderful the afternoon had been. "It was great—I loved watching you with the animals."

"Oh, thank *you*," Dr. Thayer said. "You were terrific."

"Thanks. Bye!" Monica retrieved her duffel from the kennel room and said good-bye to Ana and Jolayne. Then she tore out of Fur, Feather, and Scale and pounded down the sidewalk toward Sugarloaf Gymnastic Academy.

After twenty feet, she stopped. She couldn't waltz into class when it was half over. Emma would have her head on a plate! This time she had really goofed. Sighing, Monica turned and slunk in the opposite direction. She might as well just go home, but she had to be careful not to let anyone see her.

Quickly she turned the corner at the edge of the strip mall and cut through the parking lot. Never, ever in her life, in the four years that she had been taking gymnastics, had she ever missed a class because she just *forgot*. What was wrong with her? She'd been having so much fun at Fur, Feather, and Scale that class had completely slipped her mind. She groaned again as she shuffled along, her head hanging down. She would have to tell Emma that she'd felt sick after school and had gone home. It would be the first time she'd lied to Emma and Dimitri and all of her friends.

Monica's throat felt tight, and her eyes felt itchy. Only last month, she knew, she would never have missed a class at SGA. But last month she could still manage to do a simple squat vault.

"You are acting like a loser, Monica Celeste Hales," she mumbled to herself as she turned the corner onto her street. "A total loser. You'd better get your act together before something—I don't know what—happens."

Chapter Ten

"I'm so glad it's Friday," Candace said, plunking her lunch tray down on the Silvers' usual table. "Only half a day until we're free. Hey, you guys want to go to Gianelli's this afternoon? We can get a head start on the weekend."

"I have to go to tutoring," Maya said.

Kelly slid into a seat next to Monica. She smirked. "Oh, yeah, tutoring. I think the only thing Michael Ashton is teaching you is how to swoon when he walks into a room."

"Kelly!" Blushing furiously, Maya threw her wadded-up napkin at her stepsister. Kelly laughed.

Kathryn looked at Maya with interest. "Your tutor's cute?"

"Very cute," Kelly confirmed. "He came by the house last night to drop off some worksheets, and I saw him for the first time."

"How cute, on a scale of one to ten?" Harry asked.

"Eighteen," Kelly said, opening her milk carton.

"Whoa!" Candace cried, and the other Silvers whistled and clapped.

Her hands over her face, Maya pretended to slide down under the table. "I am going to *keel* you, Kelly Reynolds!"

"*Kill*," Kelly corrected briskly. "Short *i* sound. But enough about you," she continued. "*I* have only three hours till I have to see the Twinklers. Just thinking about it makes me depressed."

"Oh, I'm sure you're doing a fine job," Candace said, peeling the top off her container of pudding.

"And think of all the good experience you're getting," Harry added. "If you wanted to baby-sit, you could say you had lots of practice."

"Well, it's kind of harder than baby-sitting," Kelly began. Her friends didn't seem to realize just how difficult it was.

"And you sure don't get any good snacks," Kathryn joked. The rest of the Silvers laughed.

Everyone except Kelly. Why wasn't anyone taking her seriously?

"Anyway—I have an idea, Monica," Kelly said. "Why don't you come with me this afternoon? You can give me moral support and help me deal with the Twinklers, and you can also go over some of the routine for Fitness Week."

"Yeah," Kathryn said. "You only missed one day, but it wouldn't hurt to do some extra brushing up."

Monica frowned. "You mean because I've been doing the moves so lousily lately?"

"No, I didn't mean that at all," Kathryn said, looking surprised.

Sighing, Monica pulled out a plastic bag of Fig Newtons. "I'm sorry. I didn't mean to snap at you," she told Kathryn. "I'm just uptight about Fitness Week. I think maybe I shouldn't be in the exhibition."

"Not in the exhibition! Why? You looked fine yesterday," Kelly said quickly. "You were working hard, and you looked great."

"I was working hard, and I looked acceptable," Monica corrected her. "I know whether I'm doing well or not."

Silently Kelly bit into her turkey sandwich. Monica had been so touchy this past week. It was hard to say the right thing.

"Well, so do you want to come today or not?" she asked. "I'd feel a lot better if you were there." Secretly, she also thought Monica *could* use more work. Maybe if she was at SGA, she would feel like practicing. It was true that Monica's routines hadn't looked very good recently, but Kelly thought a little extra practice would fix everything.

"I can't," Monica said regretfully.

"Do you feel sick again?" Maya asked, concerned. "Is your stomach bug back?"

Blushing, Monica shook her head. She had told Emma and the others that an upset stomach had kept her from attending Wednesday's class. "No. It's just—I promised Ana I'd help her bathe some of the animals this afternoon."

"At the vet's?" Kelly asked, feeling hurt.

"Yeah. See, they really need another pair of hands, but Dr. Thayer can't afford another full-time helper, so . . ." Monica trailed off.

"How come you're so into animals all of a sudden?" Candace asked.

"I've always loved animals," Monica said. "This is my chance to be with them. You know I can't have any pets at home."

"Maybe you could make friends with the mice at SGA," Maya said, smiling. "Emma was furious this morning because a mouse chewed on some of her papers in her office."

Kelly tried to smile as the others laughed, but she felt upset. Monica was choosing Fur, Feather, and Scale over SGA. And over her.

"Maybe Julie Stiller could do something about them," Kathryn suggested. "She's catty enough."

"Meow, meow," Harry mimicked.

Everyone was laughing again, but Kelly didn't join in. She turned to Monica, pushing her lunch away. "You go there all the time," she said. "Can't you come help me for one afternoon?"

Monica looked surprised. "Well, maybe I can come by later, if Ana doesn't need me."

"So you're saying Ana is more important than I am?" Kelly felt her face flushing. She was aware that the rest of the Silvers were glancing at each other, and she felt embarrassed, but all her feelings were bubbling to the surface. "We've been best friends for two years. You met Ana two weeks ago."

"It isn't that," Monica said, frowning. "It's just—I do gymnastics all the time. It's nice to do something different, something I'm good at without so much work. I'm tired of working hard and not being very good anymore."

Five pairs of shocked Silver eyes gazed at her in silence.

Kathryn leaned forward and peered into Monica's face.

"Since when do you expect things to come easy?" she asked seriously. "Did you switch places with Candace?"

Everyone except Kelly laughed.

"Maybe it's the other way around. Maybe

80

you're not good anymore because you haven't been working very hard," she said quietly. "Did you ever think of that?"

Crumpling her paper lunch bag, Kelly stood up, tossed it into the trash, and left the cafeteria. Her thoughts were swirling like leaves on a tree. Monica was sick of gymnastics! What was going to happen now?

———

Kelly smiled determinedly as she waited for the Twinklers to change into their leotards that afternoon. It had been hard riding her bike to SGA all by herself. She'd thought that coaching would be fun, but it wasn't turning out that way. And it was a drag not to be able to hang out with her friends on a Friday afternoon. Now she was also upset from the scene with Monica. During sixth-period math they had hardly talked to each other.

Tania and Patty ran up, full of their usual energy and excitement.

"Hi, Twinklers!" Kelly greeted them, making her voice sound friendly and enthusiastic.

Soon Isabel, Maria, Ginger, and Leeza joined them.

"Hi, kids," Kelly said with a big smile. "Today we're going to learn some dance movements. Dance movements are an important part of gymnastics, because they make routines look smoother and more graceful."

"Like ballet?" Isabel asked.

"Yes," Kelly said, keeping her smile plastered on her face.

"Are we going to practice our cartwheels and somersaults?" Patty asked.

"Maybe later," Kelly answered. "First we'll try some practice balances. Now, everyone line up in a straight row here, along the edge of the mats."

After much giggling and shoving from the Twinklers, Kelly finally got them lined up and spaced out.

"Okay, everyone pick one foot up," Kelly said, demonstrating. "When you have one foot up and the other leg straight, it's called a stork position."

" 'Cause storks stand like that," said Ginger. "They're funny birds."

"That's right. Now, can everyone balance on one foot?" Kelly walked down the line of Twinklers, adjusting their feet, until they could each hold the position for ten seconds. "Good, good. You've got it!"

Next Kelly had them balance on one foot with their arms out to the sides.

"Y'all are doing excellent. Now, watch me," Kelly said. She leaned her body forward until her chest was almost parallel to the ground. Then she put her arms out to the sides and lifted one foot into the air. She raised that foot higher and higher behind her until it was above her head.

"You look like an airplane," Leeza said.

Kelly grinned. "This position is called a front scale," she said. "We use this position a lot in the floor exercise, and on the beam. I'd like you to practice it now. I'll help you."

Again she went down the line, showing each Twinkler how to get into the front scale position.

Hey, class isn't going too badly today, Kelly thought gratefully as she helped Tania raise her back leg high enough. She was trying hard to be friendly and cheerful, even though she didn't feel like it. And she was ignoring the little whisperings and gigglings among the girls. It seemed to be working. So far they were all pretty much doing what she said.

As she helped Ginger maintain her balance, Kelly was jostled from behind. She turned in time to see Leeza and Tania in a giggling and shoving match.

"Stork leg! Stork leg!" Leeza said.

Tania pushed the other little girl, trying to knock her over. "You're the stork leg!"

"Girls!" Kelly stood up and clapped her hands, trying to keep her voice even and firm. "Girls! No pushing. Come on, get back in line."

"Kelly, hellllp!" But it was too late. Ginger had been trying to hold her front scale, but without Kelly helping her she collapsed sideways into Maria, who fell to the mat with a yell.

Instantly Maria jumped up and shoved Ginger to the mat. Within seconds the Twinklers were engaged in a free-for-all.

"Twinklers! Stop it right now!" Kelly roared, stamping her foot.

Six little girls stopped dead and stared at her with round, frightened eyes.

"Why can't you guys behave just once?" Kelly cried, her hands on her hips. "You make everything so hard!"

She took a couple of deep breaths, trying to get a grip before she said something that she'd want to take back. But it was too late. First Tania's face, then Leeza's, then Ginger's crumpled into masks of unhappiness, and Kelly had a bunch of weeping Twinklers on her hands.

Oh, why isn't Monica here helping me? Kelly thought in despair. *Why did she have to go bathe animals at Fur, Feather, and Scale? Some best friend she is.*

"Hey, everyone," Susan Lu said kindly, putting her hand on Kelly's shoulder. "Kelly, why don't you get a quick drink of water?"

Her face burning in embarrassment, Kelly nodded. She knew Susan was giving her a chance to get her composure back. Leaving the Twinklers crying at the edge of the floor mats, Kelly ran over and drank from the water fountain. Then, after taking several more deep breaths, she ran back.

Susan smiled at her, patted two of the Twinklers on the shoulder, and returned to the Gold Stars.

Gently Kelly gathered the Twinklers' stiff little bodies around her so that they were all in a circle.

"Girls, I'm sorry," she said calmly. "I didn't mean to yell at you. And I didn't mean to make you cry. I'm just having a bad day. Look, let's dry our eyes and all go get a drink of water. Then we'll come back and practice somersaults and cartwheels. You guys are really good at that. Okay? Sound like a good plan? Let's go."

Still sniffling, the Twinklers shuffled over to the water fountain. By the time they'd all had a drink, they were pretty cheerful again. Laughing and chattering, they bounced back to the mats and started doing somersaults and cartwheels all over the place.

Kelly sighed. It was going to be a long class.

Chapter Eleven

When Kelly walked into the locker room at SGA on Saturday morning, she was relieved to see Monica already there. Monica hadn't quit coming to class.

"So how did it go yesterday, Kelly?" Kathryn asked. "You were worried about the Twinklers."

Kelly grimaced. "Don't ask," she said. "I'm keeping my record of making them cry at every single class. I just don't know what to do with them. I'm totally letting Mom and Dimitri down."

"You have to be firm with them," Harry advised, pulling her bobbed hair back with a headband.

"Not too firm," Candace said. "You have to be their friend first."

"Try making them laugh," Kathryn said. "Then they'll loosen up and be ready to learn."

"Try threatening them," said Harry. "Tell them you'll kick them out of the program if they don't listen."

"I can't do that," Kelly said. She glanced at Monica to see if her friend had any advice, but Monica just gave her a sympathetic glance and went back to biting a loose thread off her white unitard.

"I remember a coach I had, when I was younger than the Twinklers," Maya said. "I must have been five. She was a very famous coach, very strict. She thought I was spoiled because Dimitri was my father. So she was very hard on me. She tried to make me cry, but I never did. I wouldn't give in to her. Finally one day I decided to get her back once and for all. I put itching powder in the chalk."

Kelly gasped. "You didn't!"

Maya grinned. "I did. Then I told her I didn't understand some of the moves on the uneven parallel bars and asked her to show them. She was happy to see me admit I didn't know something. So she dipped her hands in the chalk and rubbed it in well. She did the routine, and got chalk all over her legs and arms—anywhere she had touched." Maya started laughing. "A few minutes later she was scratching all over!"

"What happened?" Monica asked.

Maya shrugged. "She knew it was me, and I got in major trouble. But she was easier on me after that."

"Well, I hope you don't do that to Michael Ashton," Kelly said, and the other Silvers laughed.

Maya snapped a hair elastic at her. "Quit talking about my tutor!"

Kelly fended off the elastic with one hand, giggling. "I remember I was pretty bratty myself when I was a Twinkler," she admitted. "We had a coach named David, and I thought he was mean, so I acted up in class a lot. I guess I was pretty unfair." She shook her head. Dealing with the Twinklers, and remembering what she had been like at that age, made her realize how incredibly patient her coaches must have been. Which meant, of course, that she needed to be more patient with her own class. She sighed.

Out in the main room, the Silvers headed over to the mirrored wall to warm up.

"Fitness Week is only ten days away," Harry said, leaning over to place her palms flat on the ground.

"It'll be fun," Kathryn said. "Plus we get out of school all day for it."

"Yay!" Candace cheered.

"I think we're all pretty ready," Kelly said, glancing at Monica out of the corner of her eye.

So far Monica hadn't taken part in the conversation, and Kelly wanted to draw her in.

"How did yesterday go at Fur, Feather, and Scale?" Kelly asked casually as she did a handstand against the wall.

Monica's face lit up. "Oh, it was super!"

Kelly felt a weight settle on her chest. She remembered when Monica used to say that about gymnastics.

"I helped Ana bathe the animals, and then I helped Dr. Thayer take the stitches out of a dog that had been spayed," Monica continued. "It was so interesting. And you know what? I even borrowed a book from Dr. Thayer about animal care."

Monica chattered on as she stretched, and Kelly watched her, feeling more depressed by the minute. It was as if Monica didn't care about gymnastics anymore—but how could that be possible? Her best friend was slipping away from her, and she had to find a way to stop it.

———

"Are you sure they won't mind my coming along?" Kelly asked after class as she and Monica walked down the strip mall to Fur, Feather, and Scale.

Monica shook her head confidently. She was

glad Kelly had asked if she could accompany her to the vet's. "No—they're really cool."

"You did okay in class today," Kelly said as they pushed through the doors of the vet's office. "You must be happy."

"Hi, Jolayne," Monica said. "This is my friend Kelly. Is it okay if we go back?"

"As if you need to ask," Jolayne said with a smile.

Monica opened the door that led to the kennel room. "Yeah, I was glad I didn't mess up," she finally answered Kelly. "But Kel, you know I'm not nearly as good as you or Maya are, or even Harry. I'm not as good as I used to be before I had this growth spurt."

"You just have to get used to being a little taller," Kelly said, sounding anxious. "Then you'll be great again."

"Maybe," Monica said doubtfully. In the kennel room, she went straight to the kitten's cage and took him out. "Look at Sam Gordon Andrew," she boasted to Kelly as she cradled him against her chest. "Doesn't he look fabulous?"

Kelly smiled and came over to pet the kitten gently. "He does look great. He's so pretty now. I'm glad you rescued him."

"*We* rescued him," Monica reminded her. "I just wish one of us could keep him."

"When are they going to put him up for adoption?" Kelly asked.

Frowning, Monica cuddled the kitten under her neck. "Probably pretty soon," she said, hating to think about it. "I'm really going to miss him. But I know Dr. Thayer will find him a nice home."

"Hey, Monica," Ana said, coming into the kennel room with a Great Dane on a lead.

"Hi," Monica said. "Ana, this is my friend Kelly. She helped me rescue Sam Gordon Andrew."

"Hi, Kelly," Ana said with a smile. "So, you're a friend of ol' Magic Hands Hales here, eh? Let me tell you, we're thrilled she puts up with us."

"Really?" Kelly smiled politely. "She's always telling me how much she loves coming here."

"We love having her," Ana confirmed. "And the animals really benefit from her attention."

"Oh," Kelly said.

The swinging door behind them opened, and Dr. Thayer came in. As usual, Monica's spirits lifted at the young vet's smile.

"Magic Hands," Dr. Thayer said. "I'm glad you showed up. I have a big rabbit in exam room two who just tried to take my finger off. Care to put on your fireplace gloves?"

"Absolutely!" Monica said, thrilled. She'd

never helped with a rabbit before. Glancing over at Kelly, she saw that her friend looked confused. "Oh, Dr. Thayer, this is my best friend, Kelly Reynolds. Remember, I told you about her."

"Pleased to meet you," Dr. Thayer said, shaking Kelly's hand.

"You too," Kelly said politely. "Monica's always talking about you."

"I was just about to say the same thing," Dr. Thayer said, laughing. "I've heard all about how great you are at gymnastics."

"Really?" Kelly looked surprised.

"Oh, sure," the vet said. "Monica and I chat while she helps me. I know all about the Silver Stars, and Emma and Dimitri—even General Lu." The Silver Stars called Susan Lu that because she could be strict sometimes.

Dr. Thayer retrieved a bottle of medicine from the locked cabinet and headed back to the exam room. "See you in a minute, Monica."

"I'll be right there," Monica promised. She hadn't realized how much she talked about SGA while she was with the doctor. Mostly she'd thought they talked about animals, and about what you had to do to become a vet.

"I'd better go," Kelly said.

"Okay. I'm glad you came with me." Monica started to pull on a pair of large suede gloves. She wiggled her fingers at Kelly. "In case of sharp fangs," she explained.

"Sounds dangerous," Kelly said, nodding. She started to head for the door, then hesitated. "I guess I'll talk to you later, okay?"

"Sure," Monica said cheerfully. She waved one large glove at Kelly, then hurried to meet her first rabbit patient.

Chapter Twelve

Emma looked pointedly at her watch. "Monica, you're twenty minutes late."

"I know," Monica puffed, out of breath from racing through the locker room and out to where the Silver Stars were practicing their floor exercises. "I'm really sorry, Emma. I'll get warmed up fast."

Emma nodded silently, then turned back to the class. "This routine will be similar to what we're doing on the beam and the vault," she said. "Each of you may choose from this list of skills. You'll perform your skill on the floor mat, then make way for the next gymnast."

Monica listened as she stretched her legs on the floor by the edge of the mat. She wished Fitness Week would disappear. She just wasn't in the mood to perform in public anytime soon.

Once she had warmed up enough, though, Monica joined her teammates. Harry ran across the mat and did a beautiful roundoff going into a back handspring. Candace did a cartwheel and a front walkover. Kathryn did a back walkover, then a back somersault.

Next to Monica, Kelly whispered, "Did you have trouble at school?"

"No," Monica admitted.

Kelly didn't say anything more but headed out onto the mat. She did a front somersault ending in a front split, then pushed up into a controlled handstand, then curled down again in a piked somersault. They were easy moves, but Monica thought Kelly did them perfectly, with total precision and control. She looked great.

Monica's turn was coming up. She decided to do a roundoff going into a straddled somersault. Many floor exercise moves began with either a cartwheel or a roundoff so that the gymnast could get power and momentum. As soon as Kelly was done she moved off the mat, and Monica began her skill. After running a few paces, she went into a roundoff, snapping her legs down hard against the mat. Immediately she bounced up into the air again, tucked her head to her waist, and grabbed her ankles with both hands. With her feet apart, she turned in the air, then straightened and landed squarely. She threw both hands in the air. Finally she had done something without crash landing!

"Very nice, Monica," Emma said with a smile. "You got great height on your roundoff. Next time try to tuck in a little tighter on your somersault. And your feet could be a little wider apart." She patted Monica's back. "But you did really well. I think you're adjusting to your height." Consulting her clipboard, Emma said, "Okay, Silvers. Go join Dimitri and the Golds for a performance overview. After that you can take a water break."

Monica stood there, panting, as the rest of the Silvers headed across the gym to where Dimitri was leading the Gold Stars through their Fitness Week routine. Emma had told her she'd executed her skill nicely but had still made two corrections. None of the other Silvers had been corrected, except for when Emma had told Candace to take the gum out of her mouth before she did her skill. Monica's face burned. What was the point of trying if she would never be good enough?

———

The week before, Monica had decided to concentrate on gymnastics again, but she was having a hard time following through. Doing all this stuff for Fitness Week was boring her. She wasn't learning anything new, the way she was at Fur, Feather, and Scale.

On Tuesday she was late because she had lost track of time playing with Sam Gordon Andrew. He had learned how to climb the wire mesh of his pen, and Monica spent time coaxing him up by wiggling a catnip mouse at the top. Seeing his fuzzy, round belly pressed against the mesh cracked Monica up.

On Wednesday Ana had called in sick, and Monica had happily replaced her in the kennel room. She cleaned all the pens, fed the animals, groomed some of them, and helped Dr. Thayer give medicine. By the time she looked at the clock it was almost five P.M. She had missed another whole class at SGA, and she felt bad about it. But not too bad. She already knew all the stuff they were doing for Fitness Week, and one more day of practice wouldn't help her do any better.

On Thursday at lunch she noticed the Silver Stars eyeing her. Kelly looked unhappy but didn't mention Monica's having skipped class the day before. It seemed as if everyone tried to talk about other things. Monica didn't mention anything that had happened at Fur, Feather, and Scale, though she was dying to tell Kelly how Dr. Thayer had helped a cat give birth to four kittens.

Still, seeing how unhappy Kelly looked made Monica decide to definitely make class on time at SGA that afternoon.

Unfortunately, it didn't work out that way.

———————

Monica rushed through the glass doors at ten minutes after four. Without even stopping to make an excuse, she raced into the locker room, threw on a leotard, and scurried over to join the Silver Stars at the uneven parallel bars. Dimitri looked at her. Monica thought he was one of the nicest coaches she'd ever met—even though he was very demanding. But today the look in his eyes made her feel embarrassed.

"Monica, class begins at three-thirty," he said softly.

"I know," she muttered. "I'm really sorry."

Dimitri seemed about to say something, but he just shook his head and motioned for Kelly to perform her skill on the uneven bars.

Kelly did two relatively easy moves, then dismounted simply.

"Monica, you go next," Dimitri said.

"Me? What should I do?" Monica asked. She hadn't come in time to choose from the list of skills.

"I'd like you to do a flying hip circle," Dimitri said.

"Okay." Monica had done this move several times. To start, she needed to hang from the top bar. After swinging back and forth several times, she would bump the lower bar with her hips. Then she would bend sharply at the hips, wrapping around the lower bar, with her legs straight. Quickly she would release her hands from the top bar and grab the lower one. She would end in a support position on the lower bar, with her body straight and her head high.

It was a fun move, one that looked flashier and more complicated than it was.

But could she still do it? It all depended on knowing where her body would hit the lower bar. If she hit too high, she couldn't bend around the bar. If she hit too low on her thighs, she might lose her balance and fall.

Walking to the uneven bars, Monica swallowed, suddenly overcome with self-doubt.

Dimitri helped her jump up to the high bar. "This skill will show off your long, slim line," he said. "It will use your long legs to an advantage. For a taller gymnast, this move looks great. For a smaller gymnast, it can look ungraceful."

Monica stared at him. Was he kidding? Was there really anything that a taller gymnast could do *better*?

With Dimitri's hands on her waist, Monica

jumped up and hung from the top bar. He let go and moved back.

"Remember," he said quietly, "you inhabit your body. It is yours with every breath, every step. You know exactly where you are in space. You see the ends of your toes. You feel the tips of your fingers. You feel the way your spine bends, and the weight of your body. You own it—it is yours. Now make it move."

Feeling almost hypnotized by his words, Monica began swinging from the top bar, first gently, then with more force. Her hips bounced against the lower bar, and all of her years of training kicked in. Everything was perfect: height, speed, position . . . she curled her hips around the bar, keeping her legs in a straight, piked position. Instantly she let go of the top bar. It seemed as if she had all the time in the world to grab the bottom bar, and she did. Then she swung in a smooth circle around and up. Finally she came to rest on the lower bar, holding it, her hips braced against it. In that moment she knew she had done the move perfectly. There would be no corrections.

"All right!" Kelly said, and started clapping.

Smiling, Monica dismounted and came over to the Silver Stars.

"Way to go, Monica," Kathryn said.

"That was excellent," Dimitri said, and Monica glowed. It had been a long time since she had done anything so well. Putting his hand on her shoulder, Dimitri added, "Emma and I would like to see you after class."

Kelly's eyes grew round. Kathryn and Harry glanced quickly at each other. Monica bit her lip.

"Okay," she said, her mind filling with dread.

———

"I'll see you later, Monica," Kelly said with a concerned look. Leaning closer, she whispered, "Call me when you get home, okay?"

"Okay," Monica whispered back. But she wasn't sure she would feel like talking to anyone. Class was finished and Monica had changed and said good-bye to everyone. Now she was headed for Emma's office. She had never, ever been called to the office before.

"Come in, dear," Emma said, looking up from her desk. Dimitri was sitting in one of the armchairs, and he smiled at Monica.

Emma gestured to the other armchair. Monica sat down.

"We asked to see you because we're concerned about your performance lately," Emma said.

Monica looked down at her feet.

"In the past two weeks you've missed two classes and been late to three others," Emma continued. "You know that isn't acceptable for a Silver Star."

Monica wished the earth would open up to swallow her. She was miserable. This was the kind of speech Candace had to sit through all the time. It wasn't for Monica.

"When you do come to class," Dimitri said, "your mind seems to be elsewhere. Your concentration is poor. Yet just a month ago, I would never have thought that of you."

Biting her lip, Monica gave a tiny nod but didn't look up.

"We know you've grown a lot this year," Emma said. "And it can be difficult to go through a growth spurt."

"I'm just too big to be a gymnast anymore," Monica blurted out, twisting her hands together. "I'm taller than all the Silver Stars. And all the Gold Stars."

"Yes, you are," Emma agreed. "But you're not taller than me, and I was an Olympic medalist. And I can think of at least four world-competition-level gymnasts who are taller than you." She named them.

"Really?" Monica could feel a flickering of hope inside. Today she had performed better than

102

she had in a long time. And Emma was telling her she wasn't too tall after all.

"But there's something else going on, isn't there?" Emma said, breaking into Monica's thoughts. "Something besides your height."

Monica sat forward in her chair. "I still totally love gymnastics. But I—I have sort of gotten interested in something else too, lately. I've been spending time with Dr. Thayer, the vet who took care of that kitten we found."

"That's terrific," Emma said, surprising her. "You're young, you should have other interests. But you need to make a choice here. Being a Silver Star requires a great deal of time and energy and commitment. Not just for your own sake, but for your teammates as well. If you can come to every practice on time and give it your all, that's great. If your head or your body is somewhere else, you should be honest with yourself and just concentrate on Dr. Thayer."

Monica stared at Emma. "You mean quit SGA?"

Emma gave her a sympathetic look. "The world wouldn't come to an end," she said gently. "We would miss you terribly, and the Silver Stars would really feel your absence. But you need to follow your heart. And lately your heart hasn't been at SGA."

Dimitri stood up and opened the door. He

smiled at Monica and patted her shoulder warmly. "Think it over, Monica," he said gently. "We know it's a difficult time for you. But you must make a decision soon. You'll feel better once you do."

Monica nodded and left the office. She wished Emma and Dimitri had chewed her out, or yelled at her or something. But for them to suggest that she quit SGA! She just couldn't believe it.

Numbly Monica hoisted her duffel to her shoulder and pushed through the glass doors. The walk home felt endless. *I never thought it would come to this,* she thought miserably. *How can I quit gymnastics? Or quit hanging out with Dr. Thayer?* That was the worst part. She just didn't think she could stand to give up either one.

Chapter Thirteen

"Come on—we haven't been to the mall in ages," Kelly coaxed Monica on Saturday afternoon after class. "We can window-shop, and eat at Mandarin Express."

Although she had asked Monica what had happened on Thursday afternoon, Monica hadn't really given her a straight answer. Now Kelly was determined to get it out of her. Taking her shopping was all part of the plan.

"I told Ana I'd help her clip a peekapoo that's boarded at Fur, Feather, and Scale," Monica said.

"You can do it later this afternoon," Kelly said firmly, marching Monica to the bus stop. "First you have to give me an hour of your time."

"Look, that is so cool," Monica said, gazing at an outfit in the window of the Gap.

Kelly glanced at it. "I'm too short for it," she said. "It would look good on you, though."

"Maybe," Monica said. "Hey, how did yesterday's Twinkler class go?"

Kelly groaned and pretended to stagger, leaning heavily against a column. "Not only am I not teaching them anything," she said despondently, "but they're actually getting worse. Now only Isabel can do a cartwheel. The rest of them have forgotten how. Either I scare them to death or I let them walk all over me."

"Hang in there," Monica advised. "They're just little kids. You're bigger than they are."

Flopping on a bench by the fountain in the middle of the mall atrium, Kelly nodded tiredly. "Yeah, yeah," she said. She'd heard it all before.

Monica sat down next to her. "Kel," she said, suddenly sounding serious. "I have something to tell you."

"What?" Kelly sat up and looked at Monica. "Are you finally going to tell me what happened on Thursday after class?"

Monica nodded. "Emma and Dimitri were so nice. They were really encouraging about the whole height thing."

"Good," Kelly said with a smile. She'd known

her mom would fix everything. Monica had performed great at class today—almost like her old self.

"They asked if there was anything else on my mind, and I mentioned Dr. Thayer," Monica continued. "Then . . . Emma and Dimitri said I needed to make a choice. That I couldn't continue with the Silvers if I didn't get my act together. I needed to choose SGA or Dr. Thayer."

"What?" Kelly yelled, feeling outraged. "How could Mom say that? I swear, if she kicks you off the Silvers, I'll quit too!" But even as she said it, Kelly knew it wasn't true. Nothing could make her leave the Silver Stars—not even Monica.

"No, no," Monica said quickly. "Emma isn't kicking me out. She only said that I needed to make a choice, and she's right. Besides," Monica added with a grin, "you know you couldn't quit the Silvers."

Kelly blushed and looked down. Monica knew her too well. "Well, anyway, how did Dr. Thayer take it when you told her you couldn't work there anymore?" she asked sympathetically.

Monica hesitated. "You don't understand," she said quietly. "I chose to stay with Dr. Thayer. I'm—I'm giving up the Silvers."

Kelly stared at her.

"I mean, I'll still come to SGA sometimes to

107

work out," Monica said in a muffled voice. "But I can't commit to being a Silver Star right now—not the way I need to."

Kelly felt on the verge of tears. "But, Monica," she said, her voice breaking. "You're fantastic at gymnastics. You've been taking it for years. How can you give it up now? How can you . . ." She was going to say "leave me," but of course Monica wasn't leaving Kelly. Just the Silver Stars.

"Look, we'll always be friends," Monica said. "No matter what. Anyway, you know I was never as good as you or Maya at gymnastics. I never will be. You guys are probably headed for the Olympics. I'm not. I don't even want to be. But I *might* have Olympic-level talent at taking care of animals. Dr. Thayer thinks I have a special touch. Maybe being a vet is my calling, like gymnastics is yours."

Monica sounded sad but also relieved not to be pulled in two directions anymore.

Meanwhile I feel like I'm going to die, Kelly thought.

"Monica," she said, "I don't want to be a Silver Star without you. But I have to be. I can't quit now. But what am I going to do when you're gone?" The first hot tears rolled down Kelly's face, and she wiped them away with her hand, embarrassed to be crying in the mall.

"You'll see me all the time," Monica said, sounding as if she was going to cry too. "At school, and after school, and on the weekends."

"But what about meets?" Kelly said. "We always share a room during out-of-town meets. You always help me with my routines. I don't want you to quit the Silvers. Let me talk to my mom. Maybe she can make an exception—"

"I don't want her to make an exception, Kel," Monica said, now crying too. "I don't want to let the team down any more than I already have. It'll be okay, you'll see. I promise."

Looking at her best friend through her tears, Kelly saw that Monica wasn't as sure of that as she sounded.

This was it. The Silver Stars were losing Monica. For good.

Chapter Fourteen

Kelly rested her head on her hands on top of Emma's desk. In one more minute she had to go out and face the Twinklers.

"Oh, there you are, honey," Emma said, coming into her office. "I just saw Tania and Patty arrive. Are you okay?" She ruffled Kelly's hair with her hand.

"Yeah, fine," Kelly muttered, even though she thought this had to be the worst Monday ever. The sun was shining in an annoying way, the birds' singing was getting on her nerves, she had gotten an A that she didn't even deserve on a math test . . . Kelly couldn't remember when so many things had felt so lousy.

"I know how you feel, sweetie," Emma said sympathetically.

"No, you don't," Kelly said, not lifting her head.

"I know you hate the fact that Monica's not a Silver Star anymore," Emma said. "But try to be happy for her. She's following her heart."

"She is not," Kelly said, looking up at her mother. "Her heart is in gymnastics. She just doesn't know it yet."

Emma smiled. "Spoken like a true gymnast. Now, you'd better get out there. Your class is waiting for you."

Moaning, Kelly flopped her head down again.

"Come on, sweetie," Emma said briskly. "It's your last class with the Twinklers before the Fitness Week exhibition. And even though it didn't turn out the way you hoped, I want you to know that Dimitri and I appreciate how hard you tried."

Glumly, Kelly stood up. A movement on the floor caught her eye as she headed for the door, and she gasped and leaped onto a chair. "Mom! A mouse!" she squealed, pointing.

Emma's head whipped around, and she took several steps backward.

On the floor, a small brown mouse raced across the floor and disappeared behind a filing cabinet.

Emma put her hand to her heart and sank down in her chair. "I hate those things," she said. "See? You're not the only one who's having a bad day. My gym is overrun with mice, I just lost one of my favorite students, I dented my car when I dropped a bag of groceries on it, I feel as if I might be getting a cold . . ." She thought for a moment. "And Dimitri's going to try to fix the wall plaster this week. And you think *you* have it bad." She grinned at her daughter.

Kelly couldn't help grinning back. "Gee, I'd love to hear more, Mom, but I have a class waiting for me."

In the gym, the Twinklers were prancing out of the locker room in their leotards. Isabel and Maria ran over to Patty and Tania, and the four of them bounced around like puppies. Patty snapped Isabel's leotard bottom. Ginger ran up and tugged Tania's hair. Leeza trotted up last and began telling a joke.

Kelly sighed. Would she have to start class by yelling at them to simmer down? She couldn't. It was her last class before the exhibition. So far, she had ruined the Twinklers. They were no more ready to perform in front of a crowd than the bunch of puppies they resembled.

Puppies . . . suddenly an idea floated into Kelly's brain. As she watched the Twinklers bouncing and playing, something that Monica had said came back to her. It was about a hurt dog that she'd helped. Monica had tried to be soothing, but had acted as if she was in charge, too. As if she was the lead dog.

It had worked for Monica.

The Twinklers were completely keyed up. Kelly figured that was because they came only twice a week, so gymnastic class was their big excitement on each of those two days. And because they were only four and five years old, the Twinklers were always crackling with energy.

Now, how could she be soothing and be the lead dog at the same time? How could she make their energy work for her?

And then it came to her—the brilliant solution to the Twinkler problem. It was as if someone had snapped up the window shades on her brain, flooding it with insight.

"I'm a genius," Kelly whispered.

Striding over to her small students, Kelly smiled. As soon as she got close, their smiles faded and their natural exuberance dimmed.

They hate me, Kelly thought, determinedly keeping her smile on her face. *They're afraid of me.* Was it too late to fix that?

"Hi, guys," Kelly said, stooping down to their level. "It's a beautiful day outside. What have y'all been doing today?"

For a moment the small girls stared at Kelly suspiciously.

Then Isabel took her fingers out of her mouth. "I went to the grocery store with my mommy," she said.

"I went to kindergarten," Tania said. "Half day."

"I played with my baby brother," said Leeza.

"I went to day care," Ginger said.

"Mommy took me to the zoo this morning," Patty said.

"I fed the ducks at the park and watched Mommy do laundry," said Maria.

"Wow," Kelly said. "You guys had busy days. Today I went to school all day. And you know what?"

"What?" Patty asked shyly.

"I'm ready to play some games!" Kelly said. "It's hard to go to school and sit still. Do y'all like to play games?"

For a moment the Twinklers were silent.

Then Isabel nodded. "I do."

"Good. I know a game. Do you know how to play Simon Says?"

"Yes," Maria cried. "I know how!"

"I thought you might," Kelly said. "But the game we're going to play is called Kelly Says. It's just like Simon Says. Can we try it?"

Six Twinklers nodded.

"Okay, everyone on the mats!" Kelly said

cheerfully. "And spread out. You don't want to poke each other in the eyes."

Tania giggled.

When the Twinklers were spread out and gazing at her expectantly, Kelly threw her hands over her head.

"Kelly says, hands over your heads!" she called.

Grinning, the Twinklers all threw their hands over their heads.

"Kelly says, touch the floor!"

Six Twinklers dropped their hands to the floor, leaving six plump bottoms in the air. Kelly smiled. So far, so good.

"Kelly says, march in a circle!" Kelly demonstrated, marching around the mat in a big circle. The Twinklers marched after her, pumping their arms and stamping in big steps.

Kelly was glad to see them use up their energy. Then suddenly she stopped and called, "Jump up and down!"

All of the Twinklers started to jump up and down, but Isabel and Ginger stopped quickly.

Kelly pointed a finger at the others and wagged it playfully.

"Gotcha! I didn't say 'Kelly says'!"

Tania, Patty, Maria, and Leeza groaned.

For the next ten minutes, Kelly continued to play a combination of Kelly Says and follow-the-leader. Leading the way, she had them walk along the very low practice beam, which was only six inches from the floor. She had them stretch up high and stoop down low. She had them jump up and down. She led them in somersaults across the mats. She had them pat their stomachs and balance on one leg.

And they did everything perfectly. After that first time, she never caught any of them again by not saying "Kelly says." They were paying too much attention, and they were thrilled to defeat her.

At the end of ten minutes, the Twinklers were thoroughly warmed up and moving like an organized machine. Kelly couldn't believe it. They were doing everything she had ever wanted them to, and doing it well. If only class could have gone like this from the beginning!

If only I *had been like this from the beginning,* she thought.

"Kelly says, make a bridge!"

Kelly showed them how, pushing up from the floor with her hands and legs. All the Twinklers made good bridges.

"Great!" Kelly praised them. "Now, Kelly says, kick your legs over your head!"

One by one, the Twinklers began to kick their legs over their heads. True, they were wobbly.

True, nothing Kelly could do or say stopped them from giggling. But two minutes later, every Twinkler had performed a beginner's backward walkover.

"All right!" Kelly cried, punching her fist in the air. The Fitness Week exhibition was saved. The Twinklers, sitting on the mats, instantly punched their fists in the air.

"Ah-ah," Kelly warned them, a huge smile on her face. "I didn't say 'Kelly says'!"

Chapter Fifteen

"Well, I guess this is it," Kelly said, looking at Monica.

Monica nodded. She was standing with her friends outside Sugarloaf Gymnastic Academy on Tuesday afternoon. Today was the first day that she wouldn't be part of the team.

"Look," Monica said. "I'll be right down the mall. Why don't you guys come get me after class, and we'll go to Gianelli's?"

"Yeah, good idea," Kelly said. She looked down at the ground and kicked some dirt against the curb.

Monica knew how upset Kelly was that she had quit the Silver Stars. It was hard on Monica too. But she was also excited. Now she could spend all afternoon at Fur, Feather, and Scale, and not worry about missing class, and not worry about being late, and not worry about letting anyone down. That felt very good.

"Okay, then," Monica said cheerfully. She punched Kelly lightly on the arm. "I'll see you in a few. Have a good class."

Kelly nodded. "See you later."

Monica's former teammates pushed through the double glass doors of SGA. Monica waited until they disappeared inside. Then she practically skipped down to the vet's. Today she didn't have to worry about messing up simple moves. Today she didn't have to worry about everyone improving but her. Today she could just have a good time.

"Monica, are you okay, honey?" Monica's mother came into Monica's room that night and sat next to her on the bed. "You've been awfully quiet all evening."

"Ummh," Monica muttered, not looking up from her English textbook.

"I'm a detective, you know," Mrs. Hales said with a smile. "It's useless to try to keep a mystery from me."

Monica couldn't help smiling. Her mother was a police detective, and she often threatened to detect whatever was bothering Monica or her brother, Gene. "It's just . . ." Monica's voice trailed off, and she shrugged.

"Was it because this was your first day away from SGA?" Mrs. Hales asked. "Did you miss it more than you thought you would? Are the Silvers disappointed in you?"

"Kelly's disappointed. I guess they all are," Monica said. "But they're trying not to show it too much. Kelly said she wanted me to be happy. She even said that something I told her about working with animals helped her deal with the Twinklers."

"Good," said Mrs. Hales. "Then what else is bothering you?"

Monica didn't want to talk about it. On the other hand, she knew talking would probably help.

"Something happened at Fur, Feather, and Scale today," she said reluctantly. "I was so happy to be there, and Ana and I were in the kennel room. Then a woman brought in her dog, which had been hit by a car." Monica's throat closed up just thinking about it. "Dr. Thayer did everything she could, but the dog didn't make it. I never even saw it. I wasn't allowed in the room. But still, I knew what happened, and I could hear the woman crying afterward. It was horrible, Mom. I guess I thought Dr. Thayer could do anything."

Mrs. Hales stroked Monica's hair. "No one can

do everything, honey," she said gently. "It must have been very sad."

"It was." Monica sighed. "It made me realize that being a vet isn't always fun and easy."

"I hate to tell you this," said Mrs. Hales, "but nothing worth doing in life is *always* fun and easy. Not gymnastics, and not being a veterinarian. If it *is* always fun and easy, then it can't be truly satisfying. It's a drag, but it's true."

Monica sighed again. "I hate these life lessons."

Mrs. Hales laughed. "And they never end, either."

Groaning, Monica flopped down on her bed. Her decision wasn't turning out quite the way she had thought.

───────

"Oh, no, what's wrong with it?" Monica exclaimed on Wednesday afternoon.

In examining room two, Dr. Thayer had asked Monica to help with a sick parrot. Wearing the long suede gloves, Monica helped the parrot's owner take the bird out of a pink baby blanket.

"I don't know!" the owner wailed. "He got outside this morning by accident, and then I found him trying to fly through the sliding glass door. He kept flying into it, bouncing off, and falling over. Now he can hardly walk. Oh, please, Dr. Thayer, can you do something? Atticus is my best friend."

The woman clutched Dr. Thayer's arm, and the vet gently dislodged her. "I'll certainly try, Ms. Cooper. Let me look at Atticus first. Monica, can you hold him upright so that I can examine him?"

Monica held the large green parrot in her gloves, praying that he wouldn't die, that Dr. Thayer would be able to help him somehow. The bird was stiff and still in her hands, his eyes closed.

"I've had him seven years," the woman said tearfully. "I try to be so careful when he's out of his cage, but he escaped somehow. . . ."

As Monica watched, Dr. Thayer listened to the bird's heart and lungs. Then the parrot opened one eye and burped. Monica's eyes widened.

"Um, did Atticus eat anything outside?" Dr. Thayer asked.

"I don't know," the woman said. She gasped. "He's been poisoned, hasn't he? Oh, my land!"

"No, not like poison," said the vet, prying open the bird's eyes and shining a light into them. "More like berries, or wild fruit. Do you have any fruit trees or bushes growing in your yard?"

The parrot's owner looked confused. "Yes, we have a wild cherry tree in our backyard. But those cherries aren't poisonous. I've eaten them my-self."

The bird hiccuped in Monica's hand.

Dr. Thayer straightened up and grinned. "Well, the good news is that Atticus hasn't been poisoned. The bad news is he's going to feel twice as bad tomorrow."

"Why?" his owner asked. "How do you know that?"

"Because he's going to have a terrible hang-over," Dr. Thayer said. "Atticus is drunk as a skunk."

"Drunk!" his owner exclaimed.

"Drunk?" Monica asked.

"Drunk," Dr. Thayer confirmed. "I've seen a few cases like this before. Birds eat fruit that's fallen onto the ground and fermented. Then they get drunk on the alcohol in the fruit."

Ms. Cooper looked at Atticus in disbelief. "He knows we don't approve of drinking," she said.

Monica stifled a giggle.

The parrot hiccuped again. "Hi, Mommy," he said in a slurred voice. "Whash for dinner?"

"Oh, Atticus," the woman said, stroking his side. She turned to Dr. Thayer. "Is there anything you can do?"

"It's not really worth treating," Dr. Thayer said. "The remedy would be just as unpleasant as

123

the illness. Take him home, give him fluids and maybe some soft bread, and let him sleep it off."

"I see." Looking tight-lipped with disapproval, the woman wrapped Atticus in his baby blanket again. "Good heavens, young man," she said severely. "Wait until your father hears about this. Drunk! My land. And barely seven years old." Still clucking, Ms. Cooper carried Atticus into the waiting room.

Monica held her laughter in until the door closed, then let it rip. She and Dr. Thayer laughed until tears came to their eyes.

"My land," Dr. Thayer said weakly. She wrote some notes on the bird's chart, then looked up at the clock. "Hey, aren't you missing gymnastics class?"

Monica shrugged casually. "I quit gymnastics."

"Whaaat?" Dr. Thayer said, her eyes opening wide.

"I just didn't have time anymore," Monica explained, taking off her gloves. "It interfered with my time here."

"Oh. Well, you know how much we all love having you here. But I'm really surprised. You loved gymnastics so much, and you were so good at it."

"How do you know that?" Monica asked.

"Just from hearing you talk about it. I know all

about Kelly and your other friends and all the competitions you've won. It was such a huge part of your life."

"Too huge sometimes," Monica said. "I mean, I have school, and coming here . . . something had to go."

"Hmm. I can certainly sympathize with that," Dr. Thayer said, washing her hands. "In high school I barely had time to breathe. I was competing nationally in tennis at that point, and missed a lot of school by being out of town. I had to go to summer school for three years. I missed my junior *and* senior proms."

"Gosh, both of them? I remember you said you played tennis," Monica said, "but I didn't realize you competed nationally."

"Sure did. Did pretty well, too. I mean, I was never going to be the next Althea Gibson," Dr. Thayer said, naming a famous black female tennis player. "But I did well. It was just about the hardest thing I've ever done, sticking with my training schedule through junior high school and high school. But now I'm really glad I did."

"Did you go to the Olympics?" Monica asked.

"No—I told you, I wasn't quite *that* good. But that didn't matter. I was good enough to go intercollegiate, and that was my goal."

"Why was that your goal?" Monica didn't understand. Didn't every talented athlete want to aim for the Olympics? All the ones she knew did.

"Because it got me a tennis scholarship to Emory University, where I studied to be a vet. My tennis talent wasn't my dream. I used my talent to *pursue* my dream."

Monica didn't know what to think. Most gymnasts at SGA were aiming for the Olympics, or at least for the world championships. Monica hadn't heard anyone talk about his or her sport as the means to achieve other goals.

"You know, colleges have gymnastic scholarships, too," Dr. Thayer said, checking a cabinet for supplies. "Even some colleges where you could study to be a vet, if you wanted. Intercollegiate gymnastics is very important."

"Really?" Monica said faintly. "That's interesting."

"And you know, Monica, if you came here just a few afternoons a week, and maybe some time on the weekend, that would be plenty—we'd really appreciate it. I'd feel as if I was taking advantage of you if you came every day." Dr. Thayer buzzed Jolayne to send in the next patient, a pregnant Chihuahua.

Monica just nodded. She felt as if someone had clobbered her head with a sledgehammer. All of a sudden she needed to rethink everything.

Chapter Sixteen

"Okay, kids," Kelly said loudly. The Twinklers, dressed in matching navy blue leotards with SGA embroidered on their chests in gold thread, crowded around her. It was Friday, and the bleachers at the Forest Park gymnasium were packed with students waiting to see the Fitness Week gymnastics demonstration.

"Remember, we're just playing Kelly Says," Kelly reminded them. "Just pretend we're back at SGA and no one is watching us. I'll tell you exactly what to do, okay?"

The Twinklers nodded solemnly. Kelly took a deep breath. Off to one side, she saw Emma nod, the signal to begin.

"Come on, then," Kelly commanded. "Kelly says, march onto the mats."

With Kelly leading the way, the Twinklers

marched proudly to the center of the exercise mats in the middle of the floor.

"And now, from Sugarloaf Gymnastic Academy," a voice announced, "Kelly Reynolds and the Twinklers!"

Kelly stopped and lined up her class. She gave them each a big smile and an encouraging nod. "First, Kelly says, do a nice line of somersaults!"

Eagerly six little girls tucked their heads under and rolled. After that Kelly asked them to do cartwheels, front scales, and backward somersaults. The Twinklers performed perfectly.

Five minutes later, each girl executed a successful back walkover, and the crowd clapped enthusiastically. Emma took the microphone and mentioned some of the benefits of beginning gymnastics at an early age. Then she gestured to Kelly.

"Kelly says, everyone take a bow!" Kelly said to the Twinklers. "You guys did great, like real gymnasts!"

Beaming, the Twinklers turned and bowed to each set of bleachers. Everyone cheered loudly and clapped.

As the Twinklers headed off the mats, Kelly said, "I'm so proud of you guys. Each one of you did her very best. I couldn't have done better myself."

Isabel stopped and faced Kelly, and her team-mates crowded around. "Isabel says, hug Kelly!"

Instantly Kelly found herself surrounded and hugged by her whole class.

"You're my favorite teacher," Patty said, bouncing up and down.

"I told Mommy I loved you," Maria confided.

"Yay for Kelly!" Ginger cried.

Happily Kelly hugged each Twinkler back. Her first coaching job had been a success after all. And she had Monica to thank for it. The only downside was that Monica wasn't here to share in Kelly's victory. And the thought of the Silver Stars performing later, without Monica, was doubly depressing. But Kelly would have to do her best—just like the Twinklers.

———

The Silver Stars weren't scheduled to go on until after lunch, at one-thirty. They had arranged to meet in the locker room at Forest Park at one o'clock to warm up and dress in their matching SGA leotards.

"Your Twinkler routine looked great this morning, Kelly," Maya said, leaning over to stretch her hamstrings.

"Thanks," Kelly said proudly. "The girls worked really hard."

"See, I told you it would be a snap," Candace said, pulling her hair into a ponytail.

"Just like baby-sitting," Harry agreed, chalking her hands.

Kelly clamped her mouth shut and didn't say anything. It *hadn't* been a snap, and it was *nothing* like baby-sitting. But there was no point in arguing with her friends. Now that there were only five of them, they needed to stick together more than ever.

"This is it, guys," Kathryn said, suddenly serious. "Our first exhibition without Monica."

"Without Monica? Who says?" said a voice behind Kelly.

Whirling, Kelly saw Monica leaning against the locker room door—wearing an SGA leotard!

"Monica!" Kelly shrieked. "What are you doing here?"

"I'm performing in the Fitness Week exhibition, of course," Monica said calmly, putting down her duffel bag.

"But—but—" Maya stammered.

"But you quit," Kathryn said.

Monica shrugged. "I changed my mind. Emma and Dimitri said I could come back. I worked on my part of the routine, and I hope to do okay. But if I don't, well, it'll just be a challenge, that's all."

Kelly ran over to Monica and hugged her

tightly. "I'm so glad you're here! Nothing's been the same without you. But what about Fur, Feather, and Scale? And Dr. Thayer?"

Smiling, Monica explained, "We've worked everything out. I'll go to Fur, Feather, and Scale on Monday, Wednesday, and Friday, and sometimes Saturday afternoon. I'll come to SGA on Tuesday, Wednesday, Thursday, and Saturday morning."

"On Wednesday you do both?" Maya asked, looking confused.

Monica nodded. "I usually have study hall last period on Wednesday, but my folks talked to the principal and got me out. So I can work at the vet's, then make class at SGA—on time."

"I'm just so happy," Kelly said, shaking her head in disbelief.

"Welcome back," Candace said, patting Monica's shoulder.

"It sounds like a really busy schedule," Maya said.

Monica laughed. "It'll keep me off the streets," she joked. "But I'll be doing two things that I love. So it'll be okay."

"That's great!" Kelly cried. "Now come on, Silvers. The *six* of us have a show to put on!"

Yelling and slapping high five, the team—together again—ran out into the Forest Park gym.

Chapter
Seventeen

"See, Monica?" Susan Lu said as Monica hung from the top uneven parallel bar. "You need to tuck up a little tighter to take care of your long legs."

Monica nodded as she watched herself in the mirror. She pulled her knees in tighter and saw that it would give her the clearance she needed to make the turn.

"It might take some extra practice, but you can make your height work for you," Susan added.

"I'm willing to work at it," Monica said happily. And she was. Looking around her, she could see the familiar hustle and bustle of Sugarloaf Gymnastic Academy. It felt great to be back. It had been the longest week of her life when she hadn't been part of the Silver Stars. Now she knew she had what it took to be part of the team.

"That's what I like to hear," said Emma, walking up in time to hear what Monica said. Monica swung down from the bar, and Emma put an arm around her shoulder.

"Welcome back," she said. "We missed you."

"Yeah," Kelly said, coming over too. "Even Beau Jarrett missed you."

Monica pretended to punch Kelly in the arm.

"I'm glad you're here for another reason as well," Emma said, pulling a cardboard box from behind her back.

The Silver Stars gathered around.

Monica raised her eyebrows at Kelly, but Kelly shrugged, obviously mystified.

"As you all know," Emma said, addressing the Silver Stars, "we've been having a bit of a mouse problem here at SGA."

Kelly groaned. "Tell me about it. Today I found tooth marks on my lunch bag."

Dimitri walked up and took the cardboard box from Emma.

"A gym cannot have mice," he declared. "Emma and I decided to hire an exterminator."

"A very qualified exterminator," Emma said.

Opening the box, she pulled out a beautiful, fluffy gray tabby.

"Sam Gordon Andrew!" Monica yelled.

The kitten meowed and wriggled against Emma's chest.

"We've decided to hire Sam Gordon Andrew to be our rodent control officer," Emma said with a grin. She plucked his claws out of her warm-up jacket and handed him to Monica. "He'll live here at SGA. And since you're our resident animal expert, Monica, we'd like you to be in charge of taking care of him. What do you say?"

For a few moments Monica was too happy to speak. She had been dreading the day when Sam Gordon Andrew would be adopted and she would never see him again. Now she would see him almost every day.

"I say, thank you so much," Monica said, hugging the kitten to her neck. "I thought I would have to give up gymnastics. I don't. I thought I was too tall to do anything. I'm not. I thought I couldn't see Dr. Thayer anymore. I can. And now I have my own pet, Sam Gordon Andrew. I just want to thank you so, so, so much." She buried her face in the kitten's fur, and he swiped at a loose strand of her hair.

Kelly clapped. "Hear, hear!"

"You're very welcome, Monica," Emma said. "We have all his pet supplies in my office. Sam Gordon Andrew is now the official SGA cat."

"All right!" the Silver Stars cheered.

"And I'll make him a special cat tree to play on," Dimitri said enthusiastically. "I have all the tools and wood at home."

Monica caught Kelly's eye, and they burst out laughing. It felt good to be home.

A GUIDE TO GYMNASTIC EVENTS AND SCORING

Calling all gymnastics lovers!

The Olympics is the hottest news story around this summer, and if you're a gymnastics fan like Kelly, Maya, and the Silver Stars, you'll probably be glued to the TV when your favorite athletes compete.

But what makes one gymnast today's superstar and another yesterday's news?

It all comes down to scoring. A gymnast can work toward the Olympics her whole career, but one measly *hundredth of a point* can make or break her.

This guide lets you in on the secrets of Olympic judging. Once you know what to look for, you and your friends can try to predict how your personal favorites will do in competition. You can cheer at their triumphs and groan at their mistakes. And you can keep track of their overall scores. You can even try to forecast the final medalists!

First, a quick overview.

The Events

Women gymnasts compete in four events: the vault, the uneven parallel bars, the balance beam, and the floor exercise. (Men compete in six events: the floor exercise, the pommel horse, the still rings, the vault, the parallel bars, and the horizontal bar.) Each event is scored basically the same, with judges looking for strength, coordination, precision, and grace.

Scoring

The judges start at 10.00 and work their way down, right? Wrong! The base score for each event is 9.40. For each error, the judges deduct fractions of a point. However, a gymnast can earn up to 0.60 in bonus points for performing very difficult skills. So the perfect score for a difficult routine would be 10.00, and a perfectly executed easier routine would score only 9.40. In 1976

Nadia Comaneci made headlines by becoming the first gymnast ever to score a perfect 10.00 in Olympic competition.

In each event, the gymnast is judged on her compulsory and optional exercises. For the compulsory exercise, all the gymnasts must perform the same routine, which was determined after the 1992 Olympics. (This year's games are the last Olympics to include compulsory exercises.) Gymnasts choose their own optional routines. In the vault only, the gymnast gets two tries at the optional exercise, with the higher score counting.

Then the six judges rate the gymnast, with the highest and lowest scores tossed out. The eight remaining scores (four from the compulsory and four from the optional) are averaged to arrive at the gymnast's final score in that event.

By keeping track of your favorite gymnast's scores, you can follow where she is in the ranking—and tell whether she has a shot at the gold medal!

Now let's take a quick look at the four events.

The Vault

The vaulting horse is four feet high, five feet long, and eleven inches wide. In the women's vault the horse is perpendicular to the runway. (In the men's vault it is parallel to the runway.) The runway is three feet wide and eighty-two feet long. Gymnasts have to run that far to build up speed!

The vault can be divided into several stages. First the gymnast explodes off the springboard, whipping her legs up over her head. Depending on the vault, the gymnast may do a half twist before hitting the horse. In the support stage, the gymnast pushes off the horse with her hands, sending her body in a high arc with a variety of twists and saltos. Finally the gymnast hits the mat with a crisp, "stuck" landing.

Things to look for: precision, height, strength, and distance. *Deductions:* Fractions will be deducted for sloppy form—unpointed toes, back too arched or not arched enough—as well as for larger errors, such as a faulty mount or a bad landing. Judges like landings to be clean and precise, without any little hops or steps.

The Uneven Bars

At their bases, the bars are three feet apart. The upper bar is about eight feet from the ground, the lower bar about five feet. The height of each bar can be adjusted slightly to fit the gymnast.

The uneven bars are the perfect showcase for a gymnast's concentration, coordination, and courage. Routines usually start on the low bar and move to the high bar. Watch for big swings on the high bar, as well as twists, handstands, regrips, and sudden changes of direction. The gymnast must perform at least two release moves, completely letting go of both bars. Judges favor routines that flow gracefully from one movement to the next and end in a strong dismount.

Things to look for: good form, crisp movements, difficult elements. *Bad signs:* slipping off the bar, incomplete or faulty moves, sloppy landings.

The Balance Beam

The balance beam is four inches wide, fifteen feet long, and four feet from the floor.

The gymnast on the beam uses acrobatic, gymnastic, and dance elements to create an exciting and harmonious routine. A performance should include several instances of at least two skills, such as a cartwheel into a back handspring, performed in a series. Required moves include two acrobatic flight elements; a turn on one leg of at least 360 degrees; a leap of great height and distance; and an element close to the beam, such as a split. A routine must last between seventy and ninety seconds.

Things to look for: changes in rhythm, a graceful blending of acrobatic and dance movements, and a strong dismount. Also, balance, grace, difficulty of skills. *No-no's:* falling off the beam (it happens!), wobbling, and not completing the required elements.

The Floor Exercise

The floor exercise is performed on a padded carpet measuring forty feet by forty feet.

In the floor exercise, the gymnast combines the athleticism of acrobatic tumbling with the theatricality of dance and music. This is the only event set to music. The gymnast must perform at least four passes from corner to corner, covering all areas of the carpet. One acrobatic pass must contain at least two saltos. Look for all passes to include moves of great height, distance, and amplitude. A routine must last between seventy and ninety seconds. Judges reward routines whose elements flow into each other smoothly and mesh well with the music. The best gymnasts incorporate both creative dance moves and difficult acrobatic skills.

Things to look for: difficulty of skills, imaginative use of the floor space, precise movements, and creative dance moves. *Bummers:* poor form, stepping off the mat, faulty or incomplete moves.

Here's an overview of the three different categories of competition.

The Team Competition

The twelve top-ranked national teams in the world compete in the Olympics. Besides determining the medals for the team competition, the events are very important because they determine who will compete for individual medals later.

Each national team has seven gymnasts. In the team competition, all seven gymnasts perform all four events. For each team, the top five scores in each event are added up. The team that earns the most points wins.

After everyone has completed the team competition, the thirty-six gymnasts who earned the highest overall scores get to compete for the individual all-around title.

Finally, the eight highest-scoring gymnasts from the team competition in each event get to compete for medals in the individual competition for that event.

Whew!

The Individual All-Around
Competition

Each of the thirty-six overall highest-scoring gymnasts from the team all-around performs a compulsory and an optional routine on all four events. Whoever totals the most points wins. That's pretty simple, no?

Individuals

Finally, the individual medals! This is what gets people's blood really pumping.

The eight highest-scoring gymnasts from the team competition in each event compete in the individual competition for that event. As in the team and individual all-around, each gymnast performs both a compulsory and an optional routine to determine her score.

And just when you thought you had a handle on everything . . .

Rhythmic Gymnastics

Since 1984 rhythmic gymnasts have competed for Olympic medals. Rhythmic gymnastics incorporates dance moves, music, and hand apparatuses to create a compelling and graceful performance. Acrobatic moves, such as aerials and handsprings, are not allowed.

The Events

Rhythmic gymnasts compete for medals in five individual events: the rope, the hoop, the ball, the clubs, and the ribbon. Individual all-around medals are also awarded.

In the group competition, teams of five gymnasts perform together in two routines. For the 1996 Olympics, teams will perform first with five hoops and then with three balls and two ribbons.

Scoring

Two panels of judges score rhythmic gymnasts. One panel judges the composition—what the gymnast does. The other panel judges execution—how well the gymnast does it.

That wraps it up! See you at the Olympics!

GYMNASTIC MOVES AND POSITIONS

Aerial: any gymnastic skill that is performed without the hands touching the floor, such as an aerial cartwheel or aerial walkover.

Back handspring: a back flip of the body onto both hands, with both legs following as a pair. The gymnast begins and ends in a standing position.

Back somersault: a backward roll on the floor or beam, with knees in the tucked position. (The aerial version of this move is called a back salto.)

Back walkover: a move made from a back-arch (or bridge) position, bringing one foot, then the other, down toward the front. Similar to a back handspring but using smoother, more controlled movements and moving arms and legs one at a time rather than in pairs.

Cartwheel: an easy move, in which the hands are placed on the ground sideways, one after the other, with each leg following. Arms and legs should be straight.

Front handspring: a forward flip onto both hands, with both legs following as a pair. The gymnast begins and ends in a standing position.

Front hip pullover: a mount used on the uneven parallel bars. The body is supported on the hands, the hips resting on either bar. Usually combined with a hip circle.

Front or forward somersault: a forward body roll on the floor or beam, with knees in the tucked position. (The aerial form of this move is called a salto.)

Front pike somersault: a forward somersault in which knees are kept straight.

Front split: a split in which one leg is forward, one back.

Front walkover: a move made from a front-split handstand position, bringing one foot, then the other, down toward the back. Similar to a front handspring but using smoother, more controlled movements and moving arms and legs one at a time rather than in pairs.

Handstand: a move performed by supporting the body on both hands, with the arms straight and the body vertical.

Hip circle: a move made by circling either bar of the uneven parallel bars with the hips touching the bar. If the hips do not touch the bar, the move is called a clear hip circle.

Layout: extending the body to its full length, usually during an aerial move.

Pike: any move in which the body is bent and the knees are kept straight.

Roundoff: similar to a cartwheel, but with a half twist and the legs standing together in a pair. The gymnast ends facing the direction she started from.

Salto: a somersault.

Somi-and-a-half: another way of saying one and a half somersault.

Sticking: refers to a dismount or final move that is performed without taking additional steps.

Straddle: a position in which the gymnast's legs are far apart at each side.

Straddle split: a split with legs out at each side. This move is used in all four women's events.

Straddle swing: a swing movement on the uneven parallel bars in which the legs are extended at each side.

Swedish fall: a move in which a gymnast does a free-fall drop straight onto the ground, with hands shooting out at the last second.

Tuck: a move in which the knees are brought to the chest.

Yerchenko: a mount for the vault, in which the gymnast does a roundoff onto the springboard.

About the Author

Gabrielle Charbonnet was born and raised in New Orleans, where she now lives with her husband, daughter, and two spoiled cats, Rufus and Fidel. She has written several other middle-grade books, as well as numerous books under a pseudonym.

When she was younger she loved gymnastics as much as the Silver Stars do.